Falling Slowly

By

Elizabeth Castle

Name: Castle, Elizabeth, author

Title: Falling Slowly

Description: Series: The Cantwell Quartet

Publisher: In The Air Publishing

Identifiers: ISBN 9781967731206 (ebook) | ISBN 9781967731213 (paperback) | ISBN 9798305268386 (amazon hardcover)

Cover Design by betibup33

Chapter One

The bar on the north side of D.C. was not the type of place one went to see and be seen. The dingy atmosphere inside lent itself more to hard drinking than to a place to socialize. Gideon Eginhard had spent many nights on the stool with the torn fabric at the dark corner table, usually nursing a single dark malt ale until fatigue dragged at him enough for sleep to seem more like a blessing than a nightmare-filled curse.

But tonight, the dank interior was about to be filled with celebration. Gideon was halfway through his drink when, in quiet shock, he watched his three friends pour in through the doors.

Nash Camhion was the first to slap Gideon on the back. "Congrats, man."

Trenton Armstrong came alongside him and punched his shoulder as he dropped into the stool next to his. "Can't believe they actually promoted you."

Isaac Brandt was third in line and dropped onto the stool opposite. "Couldn't have happened to a more deserving guy."

Gideon set down his drink. "Who told you?"

Nash brushed back the lock of his smoky hair that constantly dropped into his eyes, and his ever-present charm faded. "Better question is why didn't you tell us?"

Trenton held up his hand. "I know. He knows how ridiculous he'll look in a suit and is hiding in shame."

Isaac shoved a hand in Trenton's face. "The hardest part will be finding a suit that fits him. But we've come to celebrate the milestone of our friend, not rip on him."

"Hey, I can do both." Trenton waved the waitress over. "Three more of what he's having."

Gideon felt his mood lighten despite himself. He'd argued against the promotion, knowing there were better men for the job. But his superior had disagreed, and the promotion became fact despite his reservations. And because he felt undeserving, he had kept it to himself for as long as he could.

"So how does it feel, Detective Eginhard?" Isaac's voice overrode whatever smart-aleck comment was about to come out of Trenton's mouth.

Gideon looked at his friends, feeling their support wrap around him. "Surreal, I guess. I was trying to stay under the boss's radar."

Nash's eyes went to smoke. "Then maybe you shouldn't have put yourself in danger saving that kid."

Gideon's stomach clenched. The incident was three months old now, forgotten under the weight of all the other news stories and the short attention spans people seemed to have these days. But for Gideon, it was still a fresh memory.

Trenton kept his mouth shut. Gideon appreciated it when Trenton knew when not to joke.

Isaac, however, had a few words. "You could have been killed. You're lucky the guy had a bad aim. That bullet could have lodged in your head instead of the brick wall behind you."

Gideon took a long pull on his beer. The guy hadn't been able to aim because his other arm had been wrapped around the neck of a scrawny teenager who had been crying and trembling so hard that the man had a hard time keeping his grip. Gideon had saved the teenager from the guy who had been dealing drugs to kids behind an alley outside of a popular hangout. And hopefully saved a few others who had been there to buy the drugs that Gideon had learned were laced with a deadly dose of fentanyl. A couple of other kids weren't so lucky.

Gideon had used his superior strength and speed to take the guy down without firing a shot. The bullet that had been meant for his head missed by scant inches. It hadn't fazed Gideon at the time, though it had given him a few bad moments for several nights afterward. Even his girlfriend noticed he was more pensive than usual when he'd come home, but that hadn't stopped her from choosing that night of all nights to pick a fight. After half an hour of her yelling at him and him ignoring her, she'd stormed out of his apartment, and she hadn't been back since.

The next day, the story that ran in the paper painted him as a hero. His boss agreed. It wasn't the first time he'd been up for a promotion, but his boss made it clear that this time he wasn't going to be allowed to decline. He could either accept it or find another job. Gideon had accepted it.

Trenton's lip twitched. "His head is so hard; the bullet would have bounced off."

Gideon felt the last of his tension fade. He let out the

laugh that bubbled up. In the confines of the quartet, Gideon was known to smile, to laugh, and even to cry. The four men, four brothers, though not by blood, brought out the best in each other.

Conversation flowed easily between the men as they drank their beer, ate greasy food it was better not to look too closely at as you ate it, and enjoyed the camaraderie formed over the many years of their friendship.

Gideon looked over at Nash, the unspoken leader of their group. His full name was Ignatius Lucius Camhion, though no one dared call him that. The name was the legacy of many generations, and it was quite the burden to bear, though Nash seemed to wear the responsibility like a second skin. Gideon fondly remembered Nash punching out a classmate who called him Ignatius. The kid had regularly taunted not only Nash but a host of others, though the bully only taunted Nash when Gideon wasn't around. No one dared bully any of the quartet when Gideon was in the room. He stood head and shoulders above all his classmates. Gideon, knowing the evil that was out in the world, had made it a point to make sure his friends could defend themselves. And since no one had been around when Nash had thrown the punch, and the kid wasn't going to tell the teacher what had happened, the incident had not resulted in a suspension. But it had resulted in the bully leaving Nash and all his friends alone.

Nash had gone from a short, skinny kid to a six-foot heartbreaker before he'd turned eighteen. His hair was more charcoal than black, and that pretty, tanned face had graced many magazine covers in his late teens and early twenties. Nash had broken a few hearts along the way, but ultimately it was his own broken heart that had him hanging up his modeling career. Of the four, he was the sophisticated one: refined looks and impeccable manners. Gideon often referred to him as Prince Nash; Nash would grumble, but then usually follow that with a smart-ass comment, generally along the lines of bossing them around as if they were servants. But it was hard to remember those qualities as the beer Nash had just tried to swallow was spit out in laughter.

Gideon turned his attention to Trenton. He had been, and probably would always be, the most sensitive of the quartet, though he hid it well. Today his golden blond hair was kept a little long, locks of it falling over his forehead, but it was styled and groomed, unlike the mess it had been as a child. Trenton had been the class clown back then, always telling a joke. Today his humor was more tame, but his humor still hid remnants of the pain he'd battled in his youth that still festered inside him. No one had known Trenton's past when he'd first come to the school, but the day he'd broken down, tears and anger pouring out of him as he'd told them what had happened to him, was a day Gideon wouldn't forget. All four of them, no longer boys, but not yet men, had cried together. It was that night Gideon had talked Trenton into getting a tattoo to cover the brand on his chest that was a constant reminder of where he'd come from. Gideon, based on a dream he'd had, had drawn the red and gold phoenix that helped cover up those painful memories. The day Trenton turned eighteen, he'd gotten the tattoo as a symbol of not just rebirth, but also in honor of his friends who never failed to stand behind him. And that phoenix eventually made its way into a story Isaac wrote for Trenton.

Isaac was the brains. The overhead lights in the bar were reflecting off his gold-rimmed glasses. He was also the peacemaker and the voice of reason. He, too, was blond, but the color was more like sand. He kept it shorter than Trenton, and a hair never dared to move from its designated place. His glasses did nothing to hide the intelligence behind those lenses, but he was not one to flaunt it. In college, he'd much preferred cooking to studying, but he'd aced all his courses and had gone on to get his doctorate, and then another, and another, simply to prove to his father that he was smarter than his father was. Isaac's father demeaned those around him, so the doctorates Isaac earned were simply a much-deserved slap in the face. It had not brought Isaac any pleasure or peace. These days he had little, if anything, to say to his father. He only kept up his relationship with his mother, a woman who had been beaten down over the years by a husband who never felt she was worthy of him.

Gideon wasn't much for introspection, though the pain and guilt of the past were as much a part of him as his dark looks. But there was simply too much to do in a day to waste it worrying about the past he couldn't change. He stubbornly kept his black hair long, though regulations dictated it couldn't be past his collar. But it was long enough that most days he kept it tied back and out of the way. When he wasn't working, he still wore the battered black leather jacket from his twenties. And though his friends had joked, he did need to upgrade his wardrobe now that he carried a detective title. His uniform would now be relegated to the back of his closet, as would the street clothes he wore when undercover. He scowled, thinking he couldn't ride his Harley in a suit. His wardrobe was limited, and while he'd stopped wearing all black, the majority of his wardrobe still was, and none of it was befitting of his new title.

Thinking of his new title, he thought of his sister, Iris. No doubt she was the one who told Nash. Despite their age difference, Nash and Iris were friends. Gideon knew Iris had a crush on Nash in her youth, as so many girls did, but it had faded to friendship over the years. They were almost as close as he and Nash were. But these days she wasn't around much, as she was finishing up her last year of school.

He supposed he shouldn't be surprised Iris had told his friends. She would have known how he felt, without even having said a word. She was incredibly proud of him and the work he did, and she would champion him and tell him so. Iris called him her shield. She said he always stood between her and the evils of the world. She said it in appreciation, and sometimes with a bit of awe that made him uncomfortable.   And sometimes she said it in exasperation when she thought he'd taken it too far. He and Iris had grown up in rough neighborhoods, and she'd been shy and timid in those days, and very much afraid of the chaos and confusion around her. Gideon would have, and had, done everything he could to protect her and their mother after their father died.

Gideon's laughter stopped when he spotted Penelope

Camhion waving at her brother. Nash's face split into a grin as he rose to embrace his sister. Trenton was the next to be hugged, always was. Trenton and Penelope were two peas in a pod. Gideon knew Nash thought a romance would bloom between them eventually, but in all the years they'd known each other, romance seemed to be the last thing between them, much as it had been between Nash and Iris. Though, admittedly, Gideon had doubts that there wasn't more between them, and that they kept it between the two of them. And in Gideon's more morose moments, he secretly wished a romance would bloom between Trenton and Penny, because then maybe the intense feelings he always had around her would fade. He would never poach his best friend's girlfriend.

Gideon had known Nash years before he'd met Penelope. He vividly remembered the day they had met. As dramatic as it sounded, it had been as if the sun had come out for the first time in a long time. She'd dazzled him. She was the opposite of her brother. Her golden blonde hair and translucent skin beckoned him. But much to his dismay, her eyes had widened, and he'd seen flickers of fear in her deep blue gaze. It was a reaction Gideon was used to, though for the first time, he'd known regret. Even without the long scar across his forehead and the shorter, though no less obvious, second one that ran from below his right eye up to his hairline, he was six feet four, his mouth was in a perpetual grimace, his eyes were almost black, and his large body was muscular and intimidating. His mother told him he looked like a thug; she still did. Gideon hadn't bothered to soften his appearance, and it had stood him in good stead during his early patrol days. In some ways, when he was younger, he was glad of the scars that made his harsh appearance more so; no one messed with him or those he protected.

But for Penny, with her long blonde hair, dewy skin, sky-blue eyes, and legs for days, he longed for Trenton's golden-boy looks and fewer inches in height.

Gideon knew Penny was grateful to him, so she had quickly masked her reaction. Nash, Penny, and their parents all were grateful. He'd saved Nash's life. That day, more than any other, had changed the course of his life. And while he wouldn't change a thing about what happened that night if that meant Nash would have disappeared forever, Penny made him long for a different outcome. A different future.

A kidnapper had taken Nash outside the private school he attended. Ransom demands had been made, money exchanged, but Nash had not been returned. His family had feared the worst had come of him, though his mother had vehemently refused to believe he wouldn't be returned to them. Gideon could remember the soft feel of Victoria's ample chest under his head as she'd hugged him when she found out he had been the one to save her son; he could still smell the soft floral perfume that had smelled much like his mother's scent. As the pain receded from the medication he'd been given, he'd needed the reassurance and soft touch of a woman. She'd become a second mother to him that day.

It had been only by chance that Gideon had seen Nash when the kidnapper had been moving him to the trunk of his car, likely to be killed and dumped at a different location. Nash's mouth had duct tape over it, though Nash had been making as much noise as he could. But in that neighborhood, at that time of night people minded and attended to their own business. Nothing good happened on those streets in the dark of night. Gideon had been up to no good himself, though later when he'd spoken to the police, he'd kept that part to himself. He'd opted for the truth of what had transpired but kept the details of what he had been planning to do before he found Nash to himself. When Gideon saw what was going on, saw a boy close to his own age being tossed into a trunk as if he were garbage, his protective instincts kicked in, and he attacked the man.

Gideon, even at thirteen, had been as big as the man who had taken Nash. Gideon had gotten a good look at the man, a face that still haunted his dreams from time to time, right before the man had pulled a large knife out of his pocket. Undeterred, Gideon had grabbed a nearby broken bottle. In the scuffle, the man had lost the knife, but he had gotten a hold of the bottle in Gideon's hand. The two ragged scars on his face from that bottle were permanent reminders of that night. Bleeding and in pain, Gideon had yelled as loud as he could as he dove for the knife. The man hadn't been afraid of him; he picked up the knife and came after him once again. But Gideon's roar had been loud enough to wake the neighbors, and the man had fled into the night, leaving Nash lying in the trunk of the car and Gideon bleeding in the dirty alley.

It was at the hospital later that Gideon learned who the boy he saved was. He was the son of two very prominent figures. And while he had been too young to understand the power and influence the couple had, it didn't take a genius to figure out that these people had dough, and Nash's parents had offered him anything he wanted for saving their son. Not a complete idiot, he had taken them up on their offer, trying to think of how much money he might get out of them.

It wasn't until after he was back home in his bed, his mother's and sister's tears soaking his t-shirt as they fussed over him and his cuts, that he'd learned Nash's paternal grandfather had died trying to protect his grandson from the kidnapper. His grandfather had been picking Nash up from school, and he'd tried to fight off the man. But the older Camhion had been no match for the kidnapper, and the older man had been shot in the stomach and left to bleed out. Nash's kidnapping had been kept from the press, but a murder wasn't so easily hushed up, especially when it took place in broad daylight outside of a crowded school. The press had chalked it up to a robbery gone wrong; a punk kid thinking he could get the old man's wallet and jewelry. But Gideon knew better. He'd walked the distance to the nearest store and picked up a newspaper. The picture of the older, distinguished man on the front cover had taken all the pleasure from the windfall that had befallen him.

He'd let a murderer get away. And he was going to profit from it. At that moment, all he'd felt was guilt and anger. He'd angrily refused the money he'd been so eager to get his hands on. In hindsight, he was grateful Eldridge Camhion had talked to his mother in private, and they had agreed it was in Gideon's best interests if he accepted admittance into the private school Nash attended, to be paid in full by the Camhion family. Since he had no choice in the matter, his mother had decreed he was going to attend or else, and Gideon had vowed to be Nash's shadow during those years. He had done just that. And they had become friends.

Years later, the kid became a cop. And now he was a detective. It didn't alleviate the guilt. So when Penelope was done hugging Isaac, Gideon did what he always did when Penelope looked at him; he scowled.

Nash pulled up a stool from the other table. "Glad you could join us, but what brings you to this part of town?"

Gideon's back teeth clenched. Her style and graceful walk stood out in the dingy bar. "You have no business in this part of town."

Penny winced at the abrasive tone. "No doubt. But since this is where you hang out, and since you didn't answer me when I texted you, I didn't have much of a choice."

Gideon pulled out his phone. There were half a dozen requests from her to call her when he could. He'd heard the phone beep on and off throughout the evening, but it wasn't the sound he'd programmed for his mom or sister or work, so he'd ignored it. With his promotion came two weeks' vacation; one he wasn't too keen to take. But as with the promotion, he'd been told to take one or quit.

Trenton waved for another round. "Gideon's allergic to his phone. You'd get a faster response if you mailed him a postcard."

Gideon grunted at that, knowing it was only a small exaggeration. He was known to ignore calls unless it was an emergency. His friends and family knew to call him instead of texting him if it was urgent; otherwise, it could be days before he responded. Work took up most of his time, with his shifts often beginning or ending when it was too late at night or too early in the morning to reply.

Penny tucked her phone back into her bag. She looked dubiously at the sticky table and tucked her purse under her arm. "I need your help with something. Mom suggested I talk to you. Nash said he was meeting you here. So here I am."

Nash's eyebrow rose. "And I can't help? Isn't that what big brothers are for?"

Penny's brow rose to match is. "I need more than a pretty face."

Trenton burst out laughing and smacked a kiss on Penny's mouth. "She's got your number."

A lighthearted argument ensued, but Gideon didn't join in. Penny might not avoid him, but she had never sought him out before. He was surprised she kept his phone number handy. But something in her demeanor was off. He could see the pulse in her neck beating rapidly against her delicate skin.

Gideon's voice cut through the noise. "I'll take you home. We can talk without the dog-and-pony show."

Trenton snorted. Isaac looked offended. Nash looked bored, though his eyes were sharp and focused on his sister.

Penny nodded and rose.

Isaac yawned. "I'm ready to head out myself. Too many late nights."

Trenton patted Isaac's shoulder. "And not even because of a woman. It's sad, really. I can't wait to read your latest, stodgy dissertation on some ancient culture I've never heard of."

"At least I can read something other than a comic." Isaac hugged Penny and held a hand out to Gideon. "Congrats, buddy. You more than earned it. Maybe one day you'll believe that."

Gideon shook his hand but didn't respond to the second half of his comment. "Send your draft over. I've got two weeks to kill."

"First thing in the morning. Come on, Nash. I'm your ride." Isaac shook his keys at Nash.

Trenton mirrored Isaac and jiggled the keys to his Porsche at Penny. "And sadly, I'm going home alone. Penny, want to ditch Gideon and come take a ride with me?"

Penny shook her head. "As enticing as that is, I do need to chat with Gideon. Rain check, okay?"

Nash looked at his sister, who simply smiled at him. Then he looked at Gideon. "Take care of her. Congrats, again. Ditto to what Isaac said."

Gideon handed the waitress his credit card before Nash could. He waved his friends off. "You didn't walk here, did you?"

Penny finished her beer before she spoke. "A friend dropped me off."

Gideon nodded. Penny didn't drive much during the week. She spent most of her days navigating the city, and she said a car would just slow her down. He knew she kept a pair of sneakers in her bag. Tonight the oversized bag was missing, as were the sneakers. Her feet were in what she probably thought was a pair of practical, low-heeled sandals, but to him, they were sexy with her bare toes peeking out.

Penny glanced down to where Gideon was looking. She turned her puzzled eyes his way.

Gideon ignored the look. "Come on, I'm parked around the corner."

Penny stumbled a little as they walked to his car. "Sorry, the beer went to my head. I should have eaten first."

"Didn't want the fries?"

She shuddered. "Is that what that pile of grease was supposed to be?"

Since Gideon couldn't blame her, as he hadn't eaten any of them either, he simply took her arm to steady her while she took deep breaths of the evening air. He held the door for her. His dark blue sedan wasn't sexy like Trenton's red Porsche. It wouldn't go off-roading like Isaac's SUV. And it certainly wasn't a limousine or a town car as Nash preferred. But the non-descript sedan fit his lengthy frame. He was just glad he'd taken a moment to clean it out. When he was working, his car could get messy. On his last assignment, he'd been in plain clothes and driving his own car while he'd been part of a task force looking for a guy who'd been selling guns. The stakeout had lasted for a few days, and his car had looked it.

"I can stop and grab you something." Gideon kept his eyes on the road as he struggled to ignore the soft scent of her perfume as she sat across from him.

"I'm sure I've got something at home. You could probably do with a decent meal yourself. Didn't seem like you were any more interested in those fries than I was."

Gideon flicked his turn signal and continued to drive through the darkened roads as he headed into a nicer part of town, opposite of where he lived. Opposite of where he had grown up. "I'm sure I have something edible at my apartment."

Penny laughed. "You don't sound convincing. Come on in, and we can chat, and I can feed you in return."

Gideon pulled up in front of the two-story brick house. He remembered when she'd bought the house. The quartet had helped her move in. The aged brick was almost pink versus the red it had once been. Inside the home, the wood trim and oak railings had gleamed with a high shine. The floors were a tone deeper but had the same shine. The crystal chandelier in the entryway had grabbed his attention. His mother would have loved to have a home like the one Penny lived in, but that was far out of his reach. The two-bedroom ranch she lived in now, with worn linoleum and ancient carpet, had been all he could afford. But he'd spent hours removing the old carpet, revealing and finishing the old wood floors underneath that now gleamed like Penny's. New tile had replaced the linoleum. It would never be as grand as this house, but to him, it was home.

Penny unlocked her front door and undid the alarm. "Come on in."

Gideon reluctantly entered. Antique furniture now filled the entryway, with what was no doubt authentic antique lace curtains. However, when he followed her to the kitchen, modern reigned. "You've been busy in here."

Penny tossed her purse down onto the white quartz

counter. "Nash helped me pick it out. He's going to make some lucky girl a great husband. He has great taste when it comes to decorating."

Gideon took a seat at the breakfast bar as Penny started rummaging through the fridge. "I'm a vegetarian."

Penny pulled out a wedge of cheese, some lettuce, and tomato. "Yes, I know. Though I hear you have been known to eat fish from time to time."

Gideon tensed as she set the food down in front of him and focused her attention on him. "Only if Isaac cooks it. He's wasted in academia. He should be a chef."

Penny took a knife from the butcher block and started putting meatless sandwiches together. "Can't argue with that. Too bad you don't eat meat, though. He does some amazing things with it. What were you celebrating tonight? The guys congratulated you."

Gideon shifted uncomfortably. He'd only told his mother and sister, and he'd rushed through the announcement and refused to let them make a big deal out of it. But his sister wasn't going to let it pass. She had sent him a potted plant with huge balloons that said "Congratulations," which now sat in the window of his apartment. "I made detective."

Penny's eyes widened. "That is definitely worth celebrating. Too bad you're stuck having a makeshift dinner with me. I'm sorry, I didn't know. I'm sure you and your girlfriend had plans."

Gideon spun the plate she'd pushed in front of him. "No girlfriend. She left."

Penny laid a hand over his. "Sorry. I just remember

Nash saying you were getting serious with a new lady."

Getting serious was a major exaggeration, and Gideon wondered why Nash would tell her that. He pulled his hand out from under hers. "Not serious. Not anymore. Thank you."

Penny looked confused until Gideon gestured to the sandwich. "You're welcome."

They ate in silence, Gideon enjoying the sandwich more than any meal he'd had in a while. Fast food and protein bars on the go didn't fill a man up. But it was more the company than the food.

Gideon cleaned up their mess before she could, then turned to her. "You want to tell me why you need my help and not Nash's or Trenton's? Or even Isaac's?"

Penny's eyes held Gideon's. "I need a cop."

Chapter Two

The words sounded crazy, and the look on his face said as much. Penny wasn't sure why she'd blurted it out like that. But when Gideon went all intense, it was hard to think straight. He always had that effect on her. Over the years, she'd gotten to the point where she wasn't tongue-tied every time he was around, but occasionally she still found herself without words.

"What could you possibly need a cop for?"

Penny blushed. "Well, not a cop, per se. Mom wanted me to reach out to you about security for our fundraiser."

Gideon frowned. "That is what was so urgent you just had to talk to me? I've told Victoria many times I'm not a security expert. There are plenty of people who specialize in the kind of security her fundraisers need. I've given her several recommendations."

Her mother had told her not to take no for an answer, and to do whatever it took to get him to agree. "Didn't you just tell Isaac you had two weeks to kill? You can help with the party, and Mom will feel better. Has to be better than reading Isaac's latest book."

Gideon grunted. "I happen to like Isaac's books."

Penny could see she'd insulted him; the last thing she had wanted to do. "I'm sorry, I didn't mean anything by that."

"I realize people think I'm not smart enough or sophisticated enough to understand his writing. And I admit I prefer his fiction. But he knows how to tell a story, even ones as esoteric as his nonfiction books often are."

Penny flushed. "Honestly, I didn't mean it that way. I can barely get through one. I prefer his fiction. He knows how to weave history and science fiction in a way that's entirely unique."

Gideon changed the subject. "So why is your mom all fired up to have me put security together? She's done dozens, probably hundreds, of these parties over the years."

Penny placed a hand over her nervous stomach and went to the nearby counter where her laptop and work bag were lying. "Mom doesn't want Dad or Nash to know, but we received a threatening letter. It was slipped into the intraoffice mail. One copy made it to my desk, one to Mom's, and one to Clara's."

Gideon's eyes became alert, and he stepped forward and took the letter from Penny's trembling fingers. His lips pursed as he read it.

Penny had the letter memorized. "It's time the family paid. That's what it says. But it doesn't say who or which family member."

"These only came to the three of you?"

Penny nodded. "Clara isn't technically a Camhion. She's a Brooks. A cousin through marriage, not blood. Mom says Dad didn't get one, and Nash hasn't mentioned it. Mom is worried that maybe they did but didn't say so. Dad trusts you, and so does Nash. So maybe they would talk to you. You could find out if they received one, or if they're worried about the family."

"So your mom wants me to interrogate Nash and Eldridge?"

Penny nodded. "Discretely. But if they didn't receive one, Mom doesn't want Dad to know we received those letters. He's still sitting on a few boards, but Dad's finally relaxing and settling into semi-retirement. His doctor has warned him repeatedly that he has to slow down. Mom's afraid of what might happen to his health if he starts worrying about the family. And Nash has finally started to settle down now that he's got his own company. He might set the project aside if he knew someone had sent these letters."

Gideon sighed and took a seat. "Nash would drop it in a heartbeat. And I heard about your dad's health issues from Nash. Nash has been worried about him, too, though he's ecstatic that Eldridge turned the day-to-day business over to you. No doubt, it's half the reason Nash finally opened Cantwell's doors."

"Nash said all four of you invested in it." Nash had gotten the idea to turn Isaac's latest novel into a video game. She had wanted to invest in it as well, but Nash had told her no. Though he'd said it kindly, this one was a venture that was for the boys only. A shared passion, he said.

Gideon stared at the letter. "What was left of my savings. I've no doubt I'll see quite the return on my investment. Nash roped me into helping with the artwork. Trenton is already pulling from his archives as many photos as he can and putting scenery and storyboards together. He even made the quartet pose for some pictures."

"Do you think this guy is for real?" Penny came closer and peered down at the letter.

Gideon set the paper aside. "Maybe. It's vague. No doubt the foundation attracts some less than favorable press. Could be someone who doesn't agree with your politics."

Penny slapped her hand on top of the letter. "This isn't about politics. This is about community. How can anyone oppose the work we do?"

Gideon took her hand and rubbed the redness on her palm. "Some people would rather see destruction instead of beauty. You, your mother, and Clara have spent years and millions of dollars trying to save neighborhood parks and schools. And yes, one would think people couldn't find fault with afterschool programs and funding meals, but there will always be people out there who would rather see those communities crumble and the people who inhabit them disappear."

Penny turned her hand so that hers held his. She knew a bit about his childhood from Nash. She knew he'd grown up in neighborhoods filled with drugs, gangs, and all sorts of violence. Even in the downtrodden neighborhood, Gideon and his family had been outcasts, not quite fitting in with the rest of the people who made the neighborhood their home.

Iris had told her that their mother was a mix of Irish and Native American from their mother's side, though the Irish was hard to see. Some in the family said Gideon was the image of his Sioux great-grandfather, though there were no pictures. Iris also had dark skin and hair and favored

Gideon in her looks. As far as Iris knew, their father was of German and Indonesian descent, their grandparents having come to this country during World War II and having only one son.

Gideon's parents had been barely middle class while his father was alive, and the family had fallen into the hands of poverty after his death. Young Gideon had borne the burden of taking his father's place when he'd been too young. Penny knew Nash still felt guilty because of what had happened to Gideon during the rescue. And in those darker moments after the kidnapping, he'd confided in her that he'd do anything to help Gideon to repay what he'd done for their family. And though those early days were long gone, and real friendships had been forged, underneath there still lay a layer of guilt. Penny was not immune to the guilt either. Despite the scars Gideon bore that she would erase if she could, she wouldn't if that meant she didn't have her brother whole and well.

Gideon broke the silence but kept her hand in his. "Nash hasn't mentioned it, but I can see what I can find out. Nash, your dad, and I are going to hang out this week. And I can recommend a lab to send the three letters to and see if there are any prints or anything traceable. But this is basic printer paper, and in a plain envelope, also with your name printed out on it from a printer and not handwritten. It's unlikely we'll find anything but your prints on the paper."

"What about security for the party? Mom hired the usual people, but she'll feel better if you're there. And you don't have to wear a tux. It's an informal party, so just a suit and tie."

"Good, because I don't own one. Tell your mother I'll be there. And I'll stop by tomorrow and pick up the other two letters. Tell your mother and Clara to keep it quiet for now. I'll see what I can find. But no promises, Penelope."

Penny shivered under the intensity of his gaze. And because of the way he said her name. Her fingers tightened on his as she took a step toward him.

Gideon released her hand and took two hasty steps backward. "See you tomorrow."

Penny watched as he carefully folded the letter, trying not to touch it any more than he already had. He then beat a hasty retreat to her door and was gone before she could stop him.

Penny sighed and reset the alarm, watching him from the side window as he pulled away from the curb and headed back to wherever home was. At least she knew there wasn't a woman waiting.

And with that thought, Penny laid her forehead against the cool wood of the door. "You've got it bad, Penny."

Her voice echoed in the two-story entryway. When she'd first met him, he'd scared her. She was not exactly petite, but she wasn't a tall woman. His presence had dominated the feminine, overly decorated family room. She'd barely been able to breathe, so intense was her reaction to him. She knew the scars on his face were from saving her brother's life, and they were long healed, but that hadn't kept her from staring at them in horror. It had been a miracle he hadn't lost his eye during the fight.

Penny pushed away from the door. She admitted she'd led a sheltered life. The violence that had touched her brother, and no doubt the violence Gideon saw in his work, had no place in her well-ordered, moneyed existence, not back then nor now. Her parents had been so fearful after Nash's kidnapping and the murder of her grandfather that she'd gone to stay with her grandmother in Baltimore during the aftermath. Her grandmother couldn't remain behind after the loss of her husband, and the family felt having Penny with her as they both grieved his loss was best. She'd made friends there and had decided to stay until she'd graduated high school. She'd been home to visit often, and the family had visited her and her grandmother, but the timing hadn't been right for them to meet.

It was years after the kidnapping that she'd first come face to face with Gideon when Nash had invited him to her Sweet Sixteen party that her mother had thrown her. He'd barely spoken a word the entire time, eventually excusing himself and he and Nash disappeared, no doubt to Nash's room, where the two young men, barely out of college, wouldn't have to hear the idle chatter and laughter of teenage girls any longer.

But despite her fear, he had fascinated her. No, he didn't belong in her well-ordered world. But as time passed, as she grew older, and she hoped wiser when it came to men and relationships, she found herself drawn to Gideon. He stood up for those who couldn't stand up for themselves. Any woman he devoted himself to would find herself under his protection. That had scared her once. She hadn't wanted protection, or someone who would dominate her life, as she was sure Gideon would do.

Iris had told her often enough that she loved her brother

but needed to be on her own and away from his controlling ways. Penny had wanted to have fun, fall in love, and have a family. But those things hadn't happened yet. And fun had been nice for a while. But she was older now, and Penny couldn't help but wonder what it might be like with Gideon, to have all that masculine attention on her. And maybe protection wasn't a bad thing. She liked to think she could hold her own against him.

Smiling at her thoughts, Penny flipped the light off in the kitchen and headed upstairs. She wasn't sure when she'd started having feelings for Gideon, but spending time with him tonight had reinforced them, not lessened them.

But there was nothing she could do about him or their situation tonight. It was getting late, and she was exhausted. She wasn't overly worried about the letter, though her mother certainly was. But Penny couldn't believe anyone would wish to harm them. But as her mother had pointed out, no one had expected her brother to be kidnapped or her grandfather murdered either.

* * *

Across town, Gideon entered his apartment. No fancy alarm system here; no gleaming hardwood floors. Just utilitarian beige paint and carpet that was threadbare and in need of vacuuming. But he was so rarely home that housekeeping often fell by the wayside. His mother would admonish him, clicking her tongue at him. So for her, he at least tried to keep the apartment tidy, should she decide to stop by. And the occasional woman, he thought, though his last girlfriend hadn't stayed there often. Their fight the night she'd left for good had been only one of a handful of times she'd been over.

But tidy or not, the differences between Penny's home and his apartment were day and night. His apartment was nothing more than a place to sleep and work. He could picture her spending the rest of her life in her home, raising a family, and passing along her love of the antiques she treasured that he knew were gifts from her grandmother.

Shaking off his mood, Gideon went to his computer and booted it up. He set the letter down and pulled out the file folder he had tucked into the middle drawer of his desk. He flipped open the cover. On top was the article, now faded and yellowed behind the plastic cover, about the death of Cormac Camhion. Nash's grandfather had celebrated his seventy-fifth birthday just the week before. The paper had printed the family portrait taken to commemorate the occasion. Young Nash was smiling, all teeth and charm. Penny leaned against her mother, a younger version of the older woman. Eldridge had one arm wrapped around his wife's waist, and the other hand resting on Nash's shoulder. Cormac, too, was all teeth and charm as he smiled at the camera, the pleasure of the day on his face. Nash favored his grandfather, and one day no doubt Nash would have the same steel-gray hair.

Gideon flipped the article over. Hand-scrawled notes covered the surface of every page beneath. Names, dates, possible motives, none of which had helped him solve who had murdered Cormac Camhion and kidnapped Nash. The money had gotten lost after it had been transferred through multiple bank accounts. Today, Gideon knew the money would be easier to trace. But back then, it hadn't been as easy. The money had disappeared along with the murderer.

Gideon tapped his index finger on the stack of notes as he gazed back at the letter Penny had received. "It's time the family paid." It was vague, as far as threats went, and Gideon doubted the letter was about money owed. And while it could be a prank, in his gut it didn't feel that way. But he could be seeing things that weren't there. When one was obsessed with a murder, now twenty-five years old, it was easy to see connections that weren't there.

Gideon went back to the folder and pulled out the photocopies from the case file. His superior knew of his interest in the case and the reason why, and Gideon had pored over the files the detectives who had worked the murder and kidnapping had compiled. The case was a long time cold, and he had permission to look into it to see if he could drum up any fresh leads. So far, he had nothing more to go on than what the previous detectives had found.

Gideon flipped through the files until he found the copy of the ransom letter the kidnapper had sent to the family almost forty-eight hours after the abduction. The letter was short and to the point. The kidnapper had wanted two million dollars for the safe return of their son. Eldridge Camhion had gone to the police with the letter, and the money had been wired to the kidnapper from an account the police had set up. When another twenty-four hours had passed without Nash's return, the police working the case worried that Nash was dead and that the case had become one of body recovery.

But thanks to one teenager up to no good, Nash had lived to tell the tale.

Gideon rubbed his eyes, the numb spot around his scars a constant reminder of that night. The cold case detectives who looked over the unsolved homicide hadn't had a lead in years. They, too, knew of Gideon's interest in the case, and as a courtesy, promised to keep him appraised. In turn, Gideon had promised to do the same if he found any leads. He'd had no more luck than the half dozen detectives who had reviewed the case over the years.

Next, he pulled out the sketch the artist had made from the description that Gideon had given him the night of the kidnapping. Because the sketch had fascinated him, Gideon had learned how to draw so he could have the same talent. Over the years, Gideon had taken the sketch and updated it to make the unknown man look older, thinner, or heavier. He sketched him with different hair, beards, and even glasses.

Gideon yawned and stretched. There wasn't anything he could do about the letter tonight. Penny was safe behind her alarm system, as was Victoria. He didn't know Clara well, but he hoped she was taking precautions. He'd be sure to chat with all of them about safety when he saw them tomorrow.

Gideon photocopied the letter through the evidence bag he kept in bulk in his car. He made a few notations and slipped the copy on top of the stack of papers and put the file back in his desk drawer.

Yawning again, Gideon yanked the t-shirt over his head as he headed for bed. He caught a glimpse of his face in the mirror over his dresser. He turned his head to the light to see the scars better. He couldn't help but wonder if Penny had gotten used to the scars or if they still repulsed her.

"Damn." Gideon shoved away from the dresser and stripped off the rest of his clothes, tossing them in the laundry basket instead of the floor. He swore he could smell Penny's perfume on his clothes and his body ached simply from having been close to her. One would think he'd have gotten over his physical reaction to her. Not once had she hinted she might find him attractive. He was just grateful he had learned to keep his reactions under control until he was away from her.

Some women were turned on by his dark looks and the scars. Some were repulsed. He had no doubt which category Penny fit into. She was just too nice to stare or gawk. She was beauty and light. He was scarred and dark.

Gideon dropped naked into bed and pulled the covers over his legs and waist. Hiding his body's physical reactions didn't help, but at least he didn't have to look at it. Determined to get a good night's sleep on this first night of his unwanted vacation, Gideon closed his eyes and feigned sleep until it finally came.

* * *

Gideon strode through the offices of Camhion Enterprises. Before coming, he'd stared into his closet, wondering if he had anything that would help him blend in. A mostly useless effort when one was six-four, but he opted to wear a navy polo shirt an ex-girlfriend had bought for him and a pair of dark-wash jeans that didn't have holes or tears in them in an attempt to blend. The leather jacket had been replaced with a black windbreaker.

"Gideon?"

Gideon turned slightly to see a petite, slender woman smiling at him. Her light blonde hair fell straight down her back, and her bangs framed a perfectly oval face with unblemished, porcelain-colored skin. She reminded him of a porcelain doll his mother cherished: pale, delicate, and easy to break. "Clara."

She gave him a bright smile. "I wasn't sure you'd remember me. Penny said you were going to stop by."

Gideon watched her smile dim as he faced her. He saw her eyes dart to the scars but ignored the glance. "I never forget a pretty face."

Clara's bright smile returned. "Flatterer. I gave my letter to Penny. She should be in her office."

"Gideon, what are you doing here?" This voice was male, and one Gideon recognized at once.

Gideon waved at Nash as he exited a nearby office. "Thought I'd drop by."

Nash's dark brow rose. "You expect me to believe that?"

Gideon shrugged. "I told Penny I'd stop by."

Nash flashed his straight, white teeth. "Mom says you're taking Penny to the party this weekend."

Clara pushed her way past Nash, and her eyes begged Gideon to stay quiet.

Gideon watched as Clara walked away before facing Nash. "Ah, right. I'm taking Penny to the party."

Nash's fake smile faded. "Penny and Clara have been

acting strangely. Though with Clara, it's hard to tell."

Gideon started heading toward Penny's office and wasn't surprised when Nash fell into step beside him. "The only female immune to your charm."

Nash shrugged. "Clara never liked me, though for the life of me I can't imagine why. I try to be on my best behavior. But she turns to ice and bolts at the sight of me."

Gideon glanced down at his friend, who was watching Clara walk away. "So if charm doesn't work, try something else."

Nash jerked his head back. "Forget Clara. I've got better things to do than try to defrost her. Now tell me what it is exactly you're doing with my sister?"

Gideon heard the humor in Nash's voice, his friend's dark brow once again raised. The words rolled off his tongue, but they tried to stick in his throat. "Taking her to the party."

Nash gripped Gideon's forearm to halt him. "Not that I mind, but why?"

Why? Gideon's mind went blank. "I, ah, just am."

Nash's eyes narrowed. "Spit it out, Eginhard."

Gideon was saved from answering when Victoria and Penny came upon them.

Victoria Camhion came over, an older version of Penny, and stood on her toes next to Gideon. She kissed his cheek when he obeyed her silent command and bent down. "Penny and I were just talking about you. I'm so happy you've agreed to escort Penny to the party. It's going to kick off our charity season. This year we're hoping to raise enough funds to remodel the community center."

Penny stood still beside her mother, a faint smile on her face as she watched Gideon interact with her mother.

"Probably the only time I'll be free for one of your parties."

Victoria patted his cheek. "I hear congratulations are in order, Detective."

Gideon felt his cheeks turn pink under her proud gaze. "Thank you."

Nash stepped in before his mother gushed all over Gideon. "Guess I'd better take you shopping. Can't have you showing up at the party in your leather jacket."

Gideon scowled at Nash. "Stuff it, Camhion."

Victoria patted Gideon's chest. "You look very nice today."

Gideon felt his cheeks heat even more. His mother had taught him manners and to be kind to women and children. But Victoria had helped him navigate a life of privilege when he'd begun attending private school with Nash. Gideon doubted his mother knew or cared what fork to use at a formal dinner party. Frankly neither did he, but he hadn't wanted to embarrass the Camhion family on the rare occasions they socialized.

Gideon turned desperate eyes to Penny. "Penny, we should talk about the party."

"Yes. Mom, we'll meet up later. Nash, can you help Mom with the guest list?"

Nash shrugged and took his mother's arm. "Always happy to help a lovely lady."

Victoria rolled her eyes. "Save it for some unsuspecting woman."

Gideon laughed. "The other woman immune to your charm."

Nash kissed his mother's cheek. "She just pretends."

Penny waved them off and gestured for Gideon to follow her. "Sorry about that. I forgot about the cover story last night."

"Cover story?" Gideon closed the office door behind him so they wouldn't be overheard.

"Our attending the party together. Mom thought it might be suspect if you showed up without a good reason. She suggested I bring you as my plus one. That way no one will question why you're there."

Gideon took a seat, hoping Penny would relax. She looked tense. "You mean so Nash and your dad won't question why I'm there. You two don't think me taking you to a party would be suspicious? And what about the gossip from your friends when you're seen with me? You can't think Nash will believe I'm taking his sister on a date. He'll grill me the first time we're alone about why I'm really taking you. He already started."

Penny flushed. "Look, I realize I'm not the type of woman you'd take to a party."

Gideon cut that off. "First, I'm not the type of man you'd take to a party. And I'm not the type of man who attends a party like yours. I can't afford a ticket."

Penny sighed. "I guess Mom and I didn't think it through very well."

Gideon rose and pulled out her chair so she'd sit. "No, you didn't. I'll try to deflect Nash. But I can't do anything about the gossip if I take you."

"I don't care about gossip. And my attending with a member of our city's finest shouldn't cause a stir. And if people do gossip, then they are no friends of mine."

Gideon had to stop himself from snorting at her naiveté as she finally sat. "You can say that now in your cushy office. But I don't have a better idea, and you already told Nash. What time should I pick you up?"

Penny opened her mouth, then sagged in her seat. "I'll be there ahead of time, so no need. I'll have Mom send you the details."

Gideon squatted down in front of her, careful to keep his distance. "What's really bothering you? Did you already have a date?"

Penny folded her hands on her lap. "I don't have a boyfriend and I don't have a date. I usually go solo. Trying to find a man who is more interested in me than in my father's money is challenging. I was going to ask Trenton, but he hates parties almost as much as Nash does. And Trenton took me to the last one, so I didn't want to ask him again so soon."

Gideon knew it wasn't his place to push, but he did anyway. "So if it's not a date that's bothering you, what is?"

Penny shook her head. "I suppose I should get you the other letters."

Gideon stood when Penny rose to pull a folder out of her filing cabinet. He took the folder from her. The letters were identical to the one Penny had received. "Have there been any other letters or any other contact?"

Penny turned troubled eyes to Gideon. "Today Clara received an odd phone call from someone claiming to be a reporter asking questions about the party. Clara manages all of our publicity and social media. But he didn't ask where and why. He was asking pointed questions about who was attending. Clara thought it was odd. And Mom said she received some RSVPs from people not on the invite list. When she tried to reach out, the numbers didn't belong to the names on the replies."

Gideon pulled a notepad from his pocket and started jotting notes. "I'll need those. How about you?"

Penny wrapped her arms around her waist. "Ever feel like someone is watching you?"

Gideon stopped. "Someone is watching you?"

Penny shivered. "It's just a feeling. I ran some errands this morning, and I didn't see anyone acting suspicious. But I couldn't shake the feeling. I'm probably being paranoid."

Gideon tucked the notebook back into his windbreaker pocket. "Let's go find your mom and Clara."

Gideon didn't discount Penny's feelings that she was being watched, but he also didn't want to feed into it. Paranoia would help keep her safe, so he didn't try to comfort her. He'd been a cop for a long time, and given the circumstances and her history, it was likely she was jumping at shadows. An unsigned, printed letter delivered to the office with no other sort of warning wasn't as personal as leaving notes at someone's home or other personal property.

He followed Penny down the hall, trying not to watch the swing of her hips as she walked.

He breathed a sigh of relief when he closed the door to chat with the three women. He was now in his element as he faced the three women in his position as a police officer rather than the boy who had saved Nash.

Chapter Three

Penny kicked off her shoes as she settled back behind her desk and absently stared at her computer screen. She tried to rub the chill off her arms as she rubbed them. She knew Gideon could be blunt. She knew what he did for a living and could only imagine the things he'd seen. But listening to him tell her, her mother, and Clara what to watch and look for when out was enough to scare anyone into staying inside for the rest of their life. Even her mother, whom she thought of as indomitable, had turned pale at the real-life scenarios Gideon had laid out for them.

Her eyes focused once again at the sound of a knock on her door. The door was glass, so she waved Nash inside.

"Hey, baby sister."

Penny didn't trust the look on his face. When he looked cheerful, that was when he was up to the most trouble. "Hey, yourself."

Nash dropped down onto the seat, the black silk of his suit catching the light from overhead. "What are you thinking of, taking Gideon to the party? He hates parties. And when did the two of you suddenly become a thing?"

Penny wrinkled her nose. "We're not a thing. Mom heard about his vacation and convinced him he should come. And she thought it would be nice if I escorted him so he wouldn't feel out of place."

Nash contemplated her for a moment. "Either you're telling the truth, or you've gotten better at lying. How much convincing did it take to get him to agree to go? He's managed to avoid almost every party Mom has ever thrown."

Penny shrugged. "I asked him on behalf of Mom, and since he's on vacation, he said yes. All there is to it. He'll come, eat delicious food, enjoy my wit and charm, and then he'll go home."

Nash leaned forward. "Mom has been trying to get him to come to her fundraisers for years. Why this one?"

Penny sat up. "I already told you. He's on vacation, so he agreed to come."

Nash shook his head. "I don't like it. Something else is going on. Clara is acting more tense than usual. She didn't tell me once to drop dead today. I usually can get one or two out of her without trying. And Mom, though she hides it well, seems worried. I doubt it's the party that has her worried. And then you're going on a date with Gideon. He's my best friend, so I know better than anyone else that he steers clear of women like you."

"What do you mean, women like me?" Penny felt insulted but wasn't sure why.

"Nice girls."

Penny crossed her arms across her chest. "What's wrong with being a nice girl?"

Nash stood. "I'm sure it's crossed your mind a time or two what type of man Gideon is. People look at him and make assumptions. But what you see is not all you get. His emotions run deep. And he dates a certain kind of woman to protect those emotions. You're not it."

Penny agreed to a point. She knew Gideon hid a lot from others. Sometimes he almost seemed shy, which was ridiculous given his job. But sometimes she could sense unsureness in him. And there were times when she'd catch him looking at her, his face unreadable. At first, he frightened her: the dark hair, the scars, the gruff voice. She had made assumptions about him based on how he looked. But as she'd become accustomed to him, she thought she saw shadows of thoughts and feelings he kept hidden deep inside. And given that he'd saved her brother's life, she'd ignored her apprehension and tried to be friends, or at least friendly.

Then Penny thought of something. "Are you upset that he's taking your sister out? Is that what this is about? I can date anyone I want. I don't need your approval."

Nash waved that off. "There is no other man I'd trust more with your safety. And he could use a woman like you. A woman to show him there is a lighter side to life. But I'm afraid you'd hurt him. So I guess the reason I'm here is to see what is really going on, why you're going out with Gideon, even if it is Mom's fundraiser, and to tell you to tread lightly. I don't want to see him hurt."

Penny heard the sincerity in her brother's voice, but she couldn't imagine any scenario where she could hurt Gideon, physically or emotionally. And for some reason, his warning not to hurt him made her mad. "For pity's sake, Nash, it's just a party. He'll survive."

Penny could tell Nash wanted to say more but was

grateful when he didn't. The conversation was absurd. Gideon was not a soft, sensitive soul. And though Nash didn't know it, he would be working, so any awkward conversations, or the normal get-to-know-each-other type of date, weren't on the agenda.

Nash headed for the door. "I'm going to go find Gideon and make him go shopping. I'll see you later, Sis."

Penny turned confused eyes back to her computer. It was absurd, she told herself. She didn't have the power to hurt Gideon. If anyone were to hurt anyone else, it would be him hurting her. But despite the reassurances, she felt an odd twist in her stomach, somehow feeling Nash's words were a premonition of things to come. And suddenly all she wished for was for the party to be done and over with.

* * *

Gideon kept going through the racks of clothing, but so far nothing appealed to him. He wasn't handsome like Nash. He didn't have Nash's lean, athletic body. He was too tall and too, well, brawny, he supposed, to look good in these clothes. Nash had a sophisticated style that came naturally. He might have a fancy haircut, and his clothes were all tailored, but Gideon knew that even when he was wearing an old, faded pair of jeans and a torn t-shirt, class and breeding still clung to him.

"Jeez, man, grab something or I will." Nash stopped browsing the racks and came to stand by Gideon.

Gideon grabbed a pair of charcoal slacks.

Nash snorted. "I don't think you're a twenty-seven

inseam. Here, let me."

Gideon put the pants back on the rack. He glanced around. There weren't a lot of people in the store, and with the price tags he'd seen, Gideon wasn't surprised.

Nash brushed Gideon aside and started sorting through them himself. The pile on his arm grew quickly.

"Nash, I can't afford all that."

Nash raised a black brow at him. "I know how much money is in your investment accounts. I know what you can afford. Just think of this as an investment in your future. You need to look like a detective."

"Yeah, but not the Hollywood version."

Nash looked at the pile on his arm. "All right, try these on. Half of this probably won't fit anyway."

Gideon practically fled to the dressing room before Nash could make the pile any bigger.

Twenty minutes later, Nash was knocking on the door. "Well?"

Gideon came out of the dressing room. The charcoal slacks, this time in his size, hugged his hips and thighs but weren't too tight. They fit surprisingly well, and the black sweater he'd paired with it fit across his chest and shoulders.

Nash smiled at his friend. "Man, you clean up nice. Swap that sweater out for the light blue dress shirt and jacket to go with those slacks. And I think we've found your fundraiser outfit."

Gideon looked at himself in the mirror for a moment. There wasn't much he could do about the scars on his face, but he could do something about his hair. His mother had been nagging him that it was too long. Part of Gideon clung to the traditions of his great-grandfather and kept his hair as long as he could. But maybe it was time to put that aside. Maybe, just maybe, he could be the type of man Penny found attractive.

Two hours later, Gideon was out a boatload of cash but had a new wardrobe that would make his department proud. Nash managed to find clothes that struck a balance between not being too formal but nice enough to face the public, even a press conference if it came down to it. New jeans, new slacks and shirts, new jackets, and a few new ties rounded out his new wardrobe. And the new black leather jacket, one that didn't look like it had been through a battle, made him feel like himself.

Gideon looked in the rear view mirror as he and Nash headed toward Nash's apartment. Nash had dismissed his driver earlier, knowing Gideon would take Nash back to his apartment when they were done.

"What?" Nash glanced at his friend.

"I was thinking maybe I should cut my hair."

Before Gideon could change his mind, Nash directed him through traffic to his stylist.

An hour later, Gideon's hair was cut and styled shorter than before. His hair fell in natural waves around his face and shoulders. The best part was that his hair was still long enough to pull back if he needed to, which made him happy, but he barely recognized himself.

"You just need a fresh shave and you'll be good. My sister won't recognize you." Nash slapped his friend on the back.

Gideon heard Nash's words, and Gideon's tone took a

dark turn. "What about Penny?"

"Man, who do you think you're kidding? It's me, Nash. I'm glad you're taking your clothes seriously because of your promotion, but your hair, that's about Penny."

Gideon paid for the haircut and left a generous tip. He left the salon with Nash jogging behind him. "I don't know what you're talking about."

Nash settled into the passenger seat. "Are you going to sit here and tell me that today's transformation has nothing to do with your date with Penny?"

Gideon pulled into traffic. "It's not a date. I'm just escorting your sister to a party."

Nash wasn't fooled. "If you hear Penny tell it, she's escorting you. Planning to dazzle you with her wit and charm, I believe, while plying you with delicious food. Sounds like a date to me."

Gideon stopped at a red light and turned his dark eyes to Nash. "Your sister said that?"

"Light's green. And yes, she did. Gideon, come on. I know you better than anyone else. You've been in love with my sister since she was sixteen."

"That would be illegal."

Nash continued. "It only would have been illegal if you'd acted on it. Which you didn't. You would never take advantage of a woman like that. You are too close to your mom and sister to treat women with anything but respect."

"So now I'm a saint?"

Nash laughed out loud at that. "No, you're not a saint. But you would never take advantage of my sister. As far as I can tell, you stay as far away from her as you can. You've been fighting your feelings for years."

Gideon pulled up in front of the high-rise where Nash lived. "I don't know what you're talking about. I'm not in love with your sister."

Nash opened the door and slid out. "Yes, you are. And if you have half a brain, you'll finally do something about it before she falls for some wimpy guy who won't appreciate her the way you would. You have my blessing, if it matters. And I know my parents would approve."

Gideon kept his eyes forward. "Goodnight, Nash."

Nash shook his head. "You're going to end up a lonely old man, Eginhard. Just think about it. A little happiness wouldn't hurt you."

Gideon waited until Nash was inside the building before pulling away. Gideon was a bit perplexed by his conversation with Nash. Gideon thought he'd hidden his feelings for Penny well, but he supposed Nash was right. Nash knew him better than anyone else. Nash knew all of his secrets and had seen his dark side. But Nash knew some of what he longed for, what he'd gone without as a kid, and what he wanted, not only for his family but for himself.

And it was Nash's sister he was in love with. He should have known Nash would have guessed. His blessing? Yes, Nash did know him well, and his blessing should be the last thing he'd give. But he'd gone and done it.

His blessing. It was all Gideon could think of as he rode the elevator to his apartment, his arms laden with bags and boxes. He managed to get his apartment door unlocked without dropping his packages.

Gideon spent the rest of the night doing laundry and

pressing his new clothes. His mother made sure he was always neatly pressed when he went to school with Nash. And while the other students in the school had other people to press their clothes, Gideon had taken an odd pride in being able to do it himself.

It was around midnight when Gideon finished up his chores, checked his email, and got ready for bed. He stood at his bedroom window, gazing out into the night. A light rain was falling. He stood there for a while, watching the rain and thinking about Penny across town. Sighing at the futility of his thoughts when it came to Penny, he went to bed.

Gideon had just fallen asleep when his phone rang. Adrenaline kicked in as he turned on the lamp and grabbed his phone. His stomach knotted when he saw the caller. "Penny. What's wrong?"

Penny sounded as if she couldn't catch her breath. "I need you."

Gideon kicked off the covers and grabbed the first clothes at hand. He then grabbed his weapon and badge. "I'm on my way. Where are you? Is there anyone there?"

Penny choked out the words. "Home. Not anymore."

Gideon ran down the staircase, tying his hair back as he went, and was in his car in record time. He sped through the wet roads. The clock read two a.m., and the roads were empty. When he pulled up in front of Penny's house, the lights were off, even the front porch light. He drew his weapon as he took a look around, searching for anything out of the ordinary, any movement, but found nothing. Other than the sound of rain, it was quiet.

He was getting ready to pound on her door when it was pulled open. Penny was disheveled, her hair and clothes damp, the knees of her skirt full of mud, and her eyes red with tears. There was a scrape on her cheek. He gently pushed her back inside and closed the door behind him. He took a look and quickly figured out how to reset her alarm.

Penny was trembling when she fell against him, her arms coming around his waist. "I knew you'd come."

Gideon tucked her against his side and led her to the sofa. He tucked his weapon back into his shoulder harness. With some difficulty, he pulled her away from him and helped her to sit. "What happened?"

Penny turned up her watery blue eyes to his. "I think someone tried to kidnap me."

Chapter Four

Even in the darkness of the entryway, Penny could see skepticism on his face, or what she thought was skepticism. "I swear, I'm not making this up. I was with Trenton. We were hanging out at his house. I drove over, and Trenton walked me to my car. I decided to stop at an all-night gas station. I ran in for just a minute, and when I got back in my car, there was a man in the back seat."

Gideon's hands fisted as he listened to her story. "Did you lock your car door?"

Penny wiped her shaking hands over her cheeks. "I swear I did. I had tucked my keys into my purse after I locked the doors. I don't know how he got in."

Gideon knew there were plenty of ways to break into a car, but normally it took longer than a quick trip into a convenience store. "What happened next?"

Penny pulled at her muddy skirt. "He grabbed me around the neck from behind. He had a gun, but he wasn't pointing it at me. He was holding it up where I could see it, though. I panicked. His grip wasn't tight, so I leaned down and bit him. He swore, and I elbowed him in the face. Just like my instructor showed me. I managed to get loose and out of the car. And then I ran."

Gideon turned on the lights and took her arm. He could

see what would be a large bruise forming where her elbow had slammed into her attacker. He gently manipulated it to make sure nothing was broken. Then, now that the lights were on, he gave her another once over. "Good girl. Did you run into the store?"

Penny shook her head. "He had a gun. I didn't want him shooting the clerk. And I was afraid to get trapped. So I just ran. Thank goodness I was wearing my sneakers."

Gideon's gaze dropped from her floral skirt to her feet. Sure enough, she had on a pair of sparkly pink sneakers. "Nice shoes."

Penny felt laughter bubble up. "They were a birthday gift from Nash. He calls them my princess shoes."

Gideon responded to her momentary laughter. He then went back to her tale. "Did the man follow you when you ran?"

Penny closed her eyes, feeling tears sting her eyes again. "I could hear him swearing as he chased me. I dashed behind some apartment buildings and lost him in the alleys behind them. I didn't dare go back to my car. My phone and keys were in my purse, but I didn't grab them when I fled. I didn't know what else to do, so I walked home. I kept to side roads and out of streetlamps. As soon as I got home, I called you. I didn't know what else to do."

Gideon took her trembling hands in his. "I'm glad you called me. And I'm glad Nash insisted you have a land line. We need to go to the police department. We need to get a team to the gas station and see if we can find any evidence in your car."

Penny was only half listening when Gideon called his

boss.   She was vaguely aware of Gideon getting her a sweater from her coat closet, locking her keyless entry front door, and resetting the alarm before bundling her into his car. The trembling that had been plaguing her since she'd fled her attacker was finally subsiding as she sat in the car next to Gideon. He would help her. He would stay with her. She hadn't second-guessed for a moment that he'd come when she called.

Penny took a deep breath. "Thank you."

Gideon flashed her a quick glance but concentrated on the road. Penny could tell his mind was in cop mode.

Twenty minutes later, Gideon ushered her into an interview room. Penny took in the room. There was a table and a couple of chairs, a desk pushed to the side, and a cabinet beside it. For some reason, it wasn't quite what she expected. "This is a first."

Gideon gently pushed her into the seat of the hard chair. He then went over to a side cabinet and pulled out a first aid kit. He tore open a wet wipe and began to wipe the blood from the scrape on her face. "There are cameras in the room, and they will record our conversation. A team is headed over to the gas station to see about your car. I need you to tell me again what happened. But take it very slowly; try to remember all the details."

Penny shuddered but did as he asked, trying to ignore the feel of his fingers on her face as he cleaned and disinfected the scrape. The scrape stung, but his hands were gentle. She tried to remember how she'd gotten it but couldn't. "The man popping up behind me was shocking. I'd never had anything like that happen before. All I could think of was Nash. The man who took him had hidden in the back seat of Grandfather's car. Nash was in the front passenger seat. The man came up behind me and grabbed me by the neck."

Gideon's eyes focused on her. "Nash's attacker held a gun on your grandfather while he forced Nash out of the car by threatening to shoot him. Your grandfather tried to grab Nash and pull him back into the car."

Penny shuddered. She hadn't been there, but she'd imagined it many times. "And when Grandfather tried to stop him, the man shot him in the stomach. He lay there and bled to death in the street while the man made off with Nash. There had been a car waiting to pick them up, and they fled with my brother. This man could have had someone waiting."

Gideon once again took her hands. "Why do you think he meant to kidnap you? Why not just a carjacking?"

Penny felt tears fall down her cheeks. "I told you; it was just like Nash."

"Don't compare what happened tonight to what happened to Nash. Other than Nash, why do you think he was trying to kidnap you? What did he say?"

Penny tried to concentrate, but she was so tired. Adrenaline had kept her going, but she was crashing. Hard. "He didn't say anything. He yelled when I bit him, but he didn't actually say anything. He grunted when I elbowed him in the nose. The only words he said were when he was swearing at me as he chased me. I'd rather not repeat what he said."

Gideon let her hands go. "I can imagine what he said.

Did you see his face? When he came up behind you, did you see him in the mirror?"

Penny closed her eyes. "He was wearing a baseball cap. I think it was black. There were no logos or anything. Not a sports team or work logo. He was white. It was dark in the car, but the lights from the gas station did illuminate the interior. He had brown hair and brown eyes. His eyebrows were bushy. I didn't see anything else of his face. Just above his nose. I didn't dare turn around when I ran."

Penny exhaled the deep breath she took. "I just kept going after that. I couldn't hear footsteps except for mine. I walked the same route I drive home. I was scared, but I didn't dare stop. I wasn't sure if anyone would help me if I tried knocking. And I was scared someone might think I was a prowler or something."

Gideon took some notes. "That was a smart thing to do. It's not the best neighborhood between yours and Trenton's."

Penny shivered. "I've been to worse. But I just wanted to get home and call you. I knew you'd come. But it took me much longer to walk than I thought."

Gideon didn't respond to her comments about him. He simply started over, asking more detailed questions. After another hour of going over her story, she couldn't recall anything else. It wasn't much, and she knew it.

A knock interrupted them. A tall man with gray hair and a gray mustache came into the room. The man had an ID tag. This was Gideon's boss. "I'm sorry about what happened, Ms. Camhion."

Gideon rose but didn't let go of her hand. "Captain

Barnes."

Captain Gregory Barnes looked at Gideon. "Aren't you on vacation?"

Gideon nodded. "Ms. Camhion is a friend."

His eyebrows rose at that. "All the more reason for you to be on vacation. But never mind. The car is gone, as are all personal belongings in the car. Cell phone, wallet, etc. Our tech has gone over the security footage. No one was seen entering the car after Ms. Camhion went into the store. The perp was in the car before she stopped."

Penny's stomach dropped. "He has my wallet. My phone. He knows where I live."

Gideon's tone was matter of fact. "Chances are he already knew. If this is the same man who sent that letter, then he knows where you work, too. And your mom and Clara. I'm sorry, but discretion is over."

Penny tried to let Gideon's touch calm her, but it was no use. "But what about my dad?"

Gideon squeezed her fingers. "Your dad is stronger than you give him credit for. If anything, this might strengthen him. He has to be told. Nash, too. It might be best if you and Clara stay with your parents for a while. The three of you can finish planning the party from there."

Captain Barnes cleared his throat. "The next step is to track your activities before the gas station. The man didn't get in the car while you were in the store, so he got in it before that. Where were you before you drove to the gas station?"

Penny absently rubbed her sore elbow as she spoke. "I was at a friend's house. Trenton Armstrong. We watched movies and had pizza and beer. It's a pretty standard night for us. I went from the office to his house at about six. I was there until after eleven. I headed out and went to the gas station. It was dumb to stop so late, but I wanted to grab a candy bar. That's it. The man either got in my car at the office and sat in it for hours, or he got into it at some point while I was with Trenton."

Barnes took a seat opposite Gideon. "The two of you didn't hear anything unusual?"

Penny shook her head. "The television was loud, and we were laughing and having a good time. I didn't hear anything. And it didn't occur to me to look in the back seat of my locked car for a stranger."

Gideon tried again for a calming tone; he could tell she was getting worked up. "No one looks in their back seat, Penelope. This isn't your fault."

Penny wiped the tears that started to fall. "I thought he might kill me. But he wasn't choking the air out of me. He was just holding me still. He even took a moment to smell my hair. Gideon…"

Gideon rose and took her gently in his arms. His words were faint, but Penny absorbed the feel of him and the soothing tone of his voice. She knew she needed to pull herself together, but she had been so scared. And she didn't want to talk about it anymore.

Barnes rose. "Take a break. Then work with the sketch artist. She might have only seen the top of his face, but it's better than nothing. I'll get Armstrong's address and see if there are any security cameras."

Gideon pulled a small notebook out of his pocket and

scribbled on it. "This is his address and phone number. He'll cooperate. He's a friend."

Barnes whistled at the address written down. "Nice neighborhood. Hopefully, there'll be plenty of security cameras around. Maybe we can see the perp when he breaks in."

Gideon then wrote down another name. "I don't have her address, but you should do a wellness check on Clara Brooks. She's Penny's cousin, and she also received a letter. Mrs. Victoria Camhion, Penny's mom, also got a letter, but she would be locked up in her home with her husband. If anything had happened to her tonight, we'd have heard."

Barnes took the name. "We'll get the address and send a unit over. I'll let you know."

Penny thanked the captain but leaned on Gideon for a few more moments. She sighed and finally pulled away. "Guess we should go see the sketch artist."

Gideon brushed her hair from her face. "Not until you're ready."

Penny wiped away the last of her tears. She smiled gratefully when Gideon handed her a box of tissues. "I just can't believe this happened. I didn't think the letter sender was a threat. I guess I thought he was a harmless crackpot, getting his kicks trying to scare us. What if he had gone after Mom first? She couldn't have fought him off. What if, after he left me, he went after Clara? Gideon, we have to catch him."

Gideon took the damp tissues and tossed them in the trash. "I don't make promises I can't keep. We'll do everything we can to catch this guy. Until then, I'll make sure you, your mom, and Clara are safe. And I'll make sure Nash and your dad are safe, too. Your parents' house has top-of-the-line security and plenty of room. The five of you can get cozy for a while until we can figure out what's going on and why this guy targeted your family."

Penny took his offered hand and let him lead her from the room. Her voice was soft as they walked the poorly lit hallways. "It's been twenty-five years since Nash's kidnapping and my grandfather was murdered. The police were never able to find out who did it. What if you can't find this guy?"

Gideon stopped. "I promise I'll never give up."

Penny saw the darkness in his eyes as he gazed above her head at the closed door. She was suddenly chilled. "Gideon?"

Gideon glanced down at her. "I promise."

* * *

Gideon had paced the room while Penny worked with the sketch artist. A text came in and Clara was fine, and a unit was parked outside her house for the night. Tomorrow he'd have to talk to Eldridge about a security detail for all the women, but for now, all three were safe and sound.

When they were finally done, the artist made him a copy and left. Gideon looked into the eyes of the sketch. Caucasian, brown eyes, brown hair with large, bushy eyebrows, but that was it. Without any other features, he could be almost any man. But as the captain had said, it was better than nothing.

Gideon knew he needed to call Nash and Penny's father and tell him what happened. No doubt Trenton had already been called and was helping in any way he could. Gideon would follow up with him, but he didn't want to talk to his friend right now. He knew Penny and Trenton were close, but movie night, a few beers, and laughter could end up with a woman staying the night. Penny might not have tonight, but had she before? It tore at his gut, but he wouldn't ask. Didn't have the right to ask. So he did what he did best; he took the next steps.

Gideon brought her to the bullpen and brought a chair next to his desk for her to sit on. "We need to cancel your credit cards and call your bank. And we need to get your phone shut off. You said the perp has your wallet and cell phone."

Penny jolted. "I didn't even think of that. I had my driver's license and just one credit card in my wallet. I don't carry my bank card or any cash or anything. My phone is fingerprint-protected, so hopefully he can't get in. And I don't save my passwords on my phone. After Nash, the whole family is very conscious of how easy it is to track someone."

Gideon nodded. "Good girl."

Penny's lips curled into a small smile. "So you said earlier."

Gideon looked up, realizing what he had said. "Sorry, I shouldn't say that."

Penny laid a hand on his forearm. "I like the way you say it. Makes me feel less stupid. After Nash, everyone in the family is always so careful. We check for strangers, we watch cars that get too close, and we do background checks on everyone we work with. But it still happened anyway."

Gideon didn't want to tell her that a determined criminal was the most dangerous. If someone set out to hurt someone, kidnap, or murder them, not much stopped them. Too often it wasn't until the deed was done that anything could be done. And then, too often, it was too late for the victim and their family. But he said none of that. He took her information for her phone and credit card instead and made the calls.

The sun was starting to rise when he finally escorted Penny from the building. "You need some rest."

Penny stumbled a bit. "I'm so tired. But I don't want to wake my parents. I suppose I should go home and pack a few things to take to their house."

Gideon held open his car door. "So you'll go?"

Penny brushed her fingers over Gideon's cheek. "You said it's the safest place. So I'll go."

Gideon pulled away and gazed down at her. "Thank you, Penny."

Penny's lower lip trembled. "I should be thanking you."

Gideon drove a quiet Penny back to her house. There was a police car parked outside. The captain hadn't mentioned putting a detail on her house, but he was glad he did. Gideon did a quick perimeter check and kept Penny by his side. She undid the lock and alarm, and he closed the door behind them.

Penny stood in the entryway. "So now what?"

Gideon didn't like the paleness of her skin or the way her limbs were still trembling. "You need to rest. You're running on fumes."

Penny wrapped her arms around her waist. "I don't want to go to bed."

Gideon ushered her to the living room. "All right. Why don't you at least lie down on the couch? I'll get us something to drink, and we can just relax."

Penny nodded. "I don't have much in the way of alcohol. I think Nash might have left a bottle of bourbon. Try the cupboard above the fridge."

Gideon left her sitting on the couch, hoping she'd at least try to relax. After poking around in her kitchen, he found the bourbon and two small glasses.

Penny accepted the drink but just held it.

Gideon took a sip of his drink and set it down. He wasn't much for hard liquor and wanted to keep his head clear. "It will help you relax. And you should take off the sneakers and at least lie down."

Penny took a sip and lay on her side on the couch. She gazed down at her sneakers. She was reluctant to take them off. "You can help yourself to whatever is in my fridge. You've got to be hungry."

"Soon." Gideon grabbed the throw from a nearby chair and draped it over her.

Reluctantly, Penny's eyes drifted closed. Within a few minutes, Gideon knew she was asleep. He stepped over and removed her sneakers and tucked her legs under the blanket. He tried but failed to ignore the smoothness of her skin as he touched her calves.

Restless, knowing he wasn't ready to sleep yet, he wandered into her kitchen. He opted for scrambled eggs and a sliced apple with peanut butter. Not quite the breakfast of champions, but the carbs and protein would be good for him.

Gideon had seen much in his life. From his childhood in undesirable neighborhoods to his days patrolling the streets. Not much surprised him. But to see someone like Penny, someone who devoted her life to working hard and doing good, have something like this come into her life threw him. While he knew crime was not selective and it didn't discriminate, it seemed unfair that she was now living with this reality.

Gideon vowed he'd find the man who had done this to her, who had threatened and scared her. He wasn't sure what the man's intent was, but he'd make sure the man paid for hurting and scaring Penny.

Gideon stayed in the kitchen while Penny slept until the sun had truly risen. Penny was sound asleep, and it was the best thing for her. But he wasn't any good to her unless he got some rest as well. Thankfully, she had a recliner he could lounge in and close his eyes until she woke. The alarm was set, the officer was still out front, and the house was as safe and secure as he could make it. Gideon closed his eyes and drifted off, the scent of Penny lingering in the quiet room.

Chapter Five

"How could this happen?" Victoria Camhion held onto her daughter as she listened to Gideon.

Eldridge ran a paternal hand over his daughter's hair. "I can't believe this is happening."

Clara's voice shook as she sat on the sofa next to Penny. She'd arrived shortly after Penny and Gideon, after Penny called her on Gideon's phone, explained to her what had happened, and told her to come. "You didn't get a good look at him?"

Penny shook her head. "No. I worked with a sketch artist, but I only saw his eyes."

Nash paced the room. "Coward."

Penny sat up but kept her hand in her mother's. "He didn't seem like one."

Nash pounded his fist against his thigh. "A man who goes after women is a coward. I hope I'm next on his list."

It didn't get past Gideon's notice that Nash hadn't looked at him once since he'd come in. A brief glance at Nash's face told Gideon that his friend was furious. Gideon couldn't blame him.

But anger was not what the women needed right now. "The plan is for Penny and Clara to stay here. And I'd like you, Eldridge, to get a security detail on them if they need to go out. I'd suggest canceling the party, but I know nothing will stop you from having it."

Victoria became indignant. "No, we are not canceling it. I'm not letting this man win. We'll have our party, and we'll raise all the funds we need and more. How dare he? If he dares set foot in this house, we'll take him out."

Eldridge came and sat on the arm of the couch beside his wife. "You'll notice Gideon said he wasn't suggesting you cancel it. Though I should. I don't like the thought of dozens of strangers coming and going after what happened."

Nash pounded his fist on his thigh again. "Hundreds. We have to cancel."

Clara rose and laid a hand on Penny's shoulder in support. "We spent too much time and money on this. The money is for the youth center. If we don't raise enough funds, then we won't have a youth center to save."

Nash growled. "And you think your life, my sister's, and my mother's lives are worth it? Dad could buy and sell dozens of youth centers if he wanted. I can give you the money. Money is not the issue."

Clara stood as tall as her five feet five inches allowed. "This is about community. About the dignity of the people who live in those neighborhoods who want to preserve and care for the people and children in it. They don't want the rich, spoiled heir to the Camhion fortune to come in and save the day. This is about the future of these kids; them knowing that the community cares. It's not about you."

Nash narrowed his gray eyes on her. "And what about the spoiled heiress of the Brooks' fortune?"

Clara paled. "That's a low blow, even for you."

Penny threw a glare at Nash as she followed Clara out of the room.

Eldridge stopped him when Nash would have followed. "I think you've done enough, son. I know you're upset. And you're right. But so is Clara. She knows what it's like to lose everything. She has never liked taking charity, even when it's from her own family."

Nash rubbed his hands over his face. "I can't believe this is happening. But it should be me."

Victoria came and hugged her son. "I don't want to see anything happen to either of my children. And Gideon will see to it that nothing does."

Nash pulled away from his mother and turned on Gideon. "You. I want to talk to you."

Victoria went to her husband, and they left the room, closing the door behind them. Gideon was alone with Nash.

Nash came at Gideon and shoved him as hard as he could. Despite Gideon's size, he was knocked back several steps. Nash was used to sparring with Gideon. Nash always said that if he could take Gideon down, he could take anyone down. Gideon had enjoyed helping Nash with his training.

But right now, he knew his friend was beyond angry. He could see the red-hot flame of Nash's temper burning, but he also knew the underlying emotion was fear. So he simply let Nash shove him again and watched as Nash began to pace the room.

Nash spun and shoved his index finger into his friend's chest. "You knew. You knew they were in danger, and you said nothing."

Gideon grunted. "Your mom didn't want to worry your father. Penny and Victoria are worried about him. And they wanted to protect you. They never want to do anything that would cause you to relive those moments."

Nash scrubbed his hands over his face. "Twenty-five years and it's still there. It's rare that the memories raise their ugly heads, but they're still there. What if he had taken my sister? What if what happened to me happened to her? What would your answer have been then?"

Gideon shoved his hands in his pockets, his stomach knotted at the thought of anyone abusing Penny. His response was an honest one. "I don't know. Had someone taken Penny, I don't know that I would be standing."

Nash pulled away from Gideon. "Ah, hell, man. I've no doubt you'd be combing the streets for her if she had gone missing. You're the most focused man I know. And you always seem able to compartmentalize. Probably a good thing for a cop."

Gideon wasn't so sure, but the last thing he wanted to focus on was his own feelings. "I had warned the ladies to be on their guard. Your mom always has a driver, so I told her to make sure she wasn't out of his sight. Clara's a workaholic, and she pretty much goes from work to home and back. Penny would be the easiest to grab. She's always running around town. But this guy was bold; he tried to grab her inside her own car. The police will do everything they can. They're still looking for her car or any of her personal belongings that might have been tossed."

Nash turned dark eyes on his friend. "I want you."

Gideon shook his head. "You have to let the detective assigned to the case help. Not only am I forbidden to work for the next two weeks, I'm also too close to the family to investigate."

Nash's eyes narrowed. "That's crap. I know you, Eginhard; you'll be investigating this regardless of what your boss says. But that's not what I meant. I want you to take care of Penny. To keep her safe. I don't care if you have to tie her up and hide her in your apartment. I want you at her side until the guy who did this is found. I can't let what happened to me happen to my baby sister. And you're the guy who's going to ensure it."

It broke Gideon's heart to see the agony on Nash's face. To this day, the quartet were the only people who really knew what Nash had lived through. He'd lied to his parents; he'd lied to the therapist his mother insisted he see. He had even lied to the police. The nightmare that Nash lived through those two hellish days at the hands of his captor was there in his stormy gray eyes.

Gideon walked over and laid a hand on Nash's shoulder. He looked his friend right in the eyes. "I won't leave her side. I will do everything in my power to keep her safe. When she's not here, I'll be where she is. Okay?"

Nash nodded and blinked away the moisture in his eyes. "What are the next steps?"

Gideon glanced at the closed door. "First step is to get Penelope's cooperation. The fright from last night will keep her compliant for a day or two, but it won't last. She's headstrong, like her brother."

Nash rubbed his palms over his eyes, rubbing away the

tears that had snuck up on him. "That she is. She's a fighter, too. And she's smart. Want me to talk to her?"

It would be the easiest thing for him to say yes and let Nash talk to Penny. But if he were going to protect her, he needed to be the one to talk to her. And perhaps if he could get accustomed to her presence, the ache in his heart when he was around her would fade.

Gideon squeezed Nash's shoulder in support. "I'll talk to her. You have amends to make."

Nash swore. "It's not like she'd accept my apology anyway. I don't know what it is about Clara, but she drives me mad. All that self-control is not normal. I don't think I've ever seen her laugh, or cry, or any normal female emotions."

Gideon refrained from telling Nash he had. Well, except maybe the cry part. Clara was usually friendly, but she clearly didn't like Nash. Gideon didn't know why, but it had always been that way as far as he knew.

A soft tap at the door had both men turning. Gideon spoke, "It's safe to come in, Penny."

Penny eased her face through the doorway before coming in.

Nash laughed. "I need to learn to do that. How did you know it was Penny knocking?"

Gideon refrained from telling him what he couldn't articulate. He just knew when she was nearby. "Nash?"

Nash nodded. "Good luck."

Penny leaned against the wooden door after Nash left. "Good luck with what?"

Gideon took a seat on the sofa, hoping that by not

towering over her she'd be more inclined to listen to reason. "Nash would like to put your safety in my hands."

Penny closed her eyes for a moment. They were a stormy blue when she opened them. "Of course he does. But I'm sure you have better things to do on your only vacation in years than babysitting me. I'm safe behind these walls."

Gideon watched her until she threw up her hands.

"Okay, okay. I know. I'm not one to sit still. But I won't have you give up your free time for me."

Gideon looked her in the eyes. "You don't get a choice. And neither do I. I'll pick you up here and take you to work if you don't drive in with your mother. I'll chauffeur you to whatever meetings you have. You have a doctor's appointment; I'll be there. You need to go shopping; I'll be there. You have a date; I'll be there."

Penny dropped onto the opposite sofa. "Very romantic, I'm sure. He'd take one look at you and run in the other direction."

Gideon shrugged, ignoring the hurt her words caused. "Until we find this guy, I'm your shadow, whether you like it or not."

Penny dropped her gaze. "I know I should be grateful and just say thank you. And I was the one who called you last night."

Gideon rose. "It's only temporary. We'll catch him and your life can go back to normal. I'll need your schedule for the rest of the week. I've got some personal things to attend to, so I'll need to coordinate them with your schedule."

Penny came toward him. "I was really scared last night."

Gideon went still when Penny wrapped her arms around him and hugged him. He could feel the light tremors in her limbs as their bodies touched. He couldn't recall a time when Penny had ever hugged him, with the exception of last night. With the smell of her hair in his nostrils and the feel of her soft breasts against his chest, it was a miracle he remembered his own name.

Gideon struggled against the urge to wrap his arms around her and offer her the comfort she sought.

The door swung open, and Nash strolled in. "Man, that woman is stubborn."

Gideon took a hasty step away from Penny and almost fell back onto the sofa. Only fast reflexes kept him on his feet.

Penny looked up and turned to see Nash. Her eyes were filled with unshed tears as she crossed to her brother. Nash held his arms open to her.

Gideon watched brother and sister embrace. Nash simply looked at him, the message clear in his eyes. Nothing had better happen to his sister. Gideon tipped his head and left.

* * *

Gideon made sure the ladies were staying put for the rest of the day before he left the Camhion's home. In his street clothes, he headed to the precinct. In the dimly lit hallways of the worn police station, he felt himself relaxing. Being in the Camhion home always made him uncomfortable, no matter how often he had been there. The elegance and opulence of the home weren't something he could get used to. He could relax in his apartment, surrounded by the minimal furniture that had seen better days. He could truly relax in his mother's home, surrounded by the scents and memories of his childhood.

Oddly, the old station was as much a part of him as his mother's home. He nodded to people he knew as he made his way to his desk. He knew the lab would still be going through security footage. Without Penny's car, there wouldn't be any physical evidence. But he hoped somewhere between her office, Trenton's house, and the gas station, they'd get a good look at the guy. There was a BOLO out for her car, but he wasn't holding out hope. He could only hope there would be something soon. The attempted kidnapping of the daughter of one of the most influential men in town would get priority over some of the other cases. But without forensics, fingerprints, or any other evidence besides Penny's account of the attack, there wasn't much to go on.

"Gideon."

Gideon looked up and saw a disheveled Trenton. His hair was unkempt and his pants wrinkled. It was obvious he hadn't slept and was wearing yesterday's clothes. Gideon knew Trenton had been thoroughly questioned last night. The detective in charge of the case would have made Trenton's home his second stop, right after all the evidence had been collected at the gas station.

Gideon gestured for Trenton to come over to his desk. "You were next on my list after the precinct."

"I knew you'd be here. Figured I'd save you the trip. And

I was curious if there had been any other leads since last night. But the detective said nothing new has developed in the past few hours. Suppose it was too much to hope for this early in the investigation."

Gideon declined to state the statistics of solving crimes when there were no leads from the outset of an investigation. But with kidnappings and homicides, the longer the clock ticked, the less likely the culprit would be found. "I read your report already, but I'd like you to go over it again for me."

Trenton dropped into the seat across from Gideon, a hand covering a huge yawn. "There really isn't much to tell. Penny came over for dinner and a movie. She arrived at my house between 6:00 and 6:30 after she left work. It's not unusual for her to come over when neither of us has other entertainment lined up."

Gideon's jaw clenched. "You mean a date."

Trenton shrugged. "Yeah. Our Friday night date night is long-standing. If neither of us has plans, she'll come over to my place. Usually, we have dinner, split a bottle of wine, or have a couple of beers, and watch whatever catches our fancy. Last night she was in the mood for a comedy. Dinner and beer were done by eight, and the movie was done around eleven. I walked her out to her car. I didn't see anything, and her car didn't appear to be tampered with. She unlocked it and left."

Gideon wanted to ask why their movie took three hours to watch but knew he might not like the answer to that question. Trenton was a real charmer, and Penny clearly wasn't immune. He'd seen the pair together many times;

they would cozy up, chat, and laugh, their heads bent intimately so no one else could hear what they were saying, and then head out for the night.

Trenton snapped his fingers in front of Gideon's face. "Awake, pal? You look worse than I do. I didn't sleep after the visit from the detective. I called Penny, but I got her voicemail. The detective said she was with you. I texted Nash a little while ago, and he said she's holed up at her folks. Be honest with me, Gideon. Can you catch this guy?"

Gideon was silent for a moment. "Truth? I don't know. The women said they had received some threatening letters. But there was no evidence to be found, and the letters were not that threatening. There were no overt threats and nothing specific to any one person. Penny is now convinced the person who did it is the person who took Nash. But the likelihood of that is slim at best."

Trenton leaned back and crossed his ankle over his knee. "I imagine Nash is thinking the same thing. It seems unlikely that two people in the same family would be targets of kidnapping."

Gideon disagreed. "Any other family, sure. But this is the Camhion family we're talking about. They command a lot of power in this town and have a lot of money. Eldridge controls a massive fortune; he rubs elbows with politicians and dignitaries. He's on the board of several foundations and businesses. He's the name people wish were on their guest list. And Nash and Penny are prime targets. Clara is not as big a target, but she could still be in danger. And there is nothing Eldridge wouldn't do if anyone came near Victoria."

Trenton considered that. "Does sound like quite a pool of suspects to choose from. Could be anyone."

Gideon nodded, but deep in his gut, this felt personal. When Nash was kidnapped, Cormac's murder was not necessary. The kidnapper could have overpowered the man instead of shooting him. And Nash could have been grabbed any number of times during the day without so many witnesses. The fact that Cormac was shot while Nash was grabbed never felt random to him. And given what Nash went through at the hands of the kidnapper, the man who had taken him was one sick bastard. The thought that Penny might have endured even a fraction of what Nash had made him feel sick. And if he felt that way, he could easily imagine how Nash was feeling right now.

Trenton continued, oblivious to Gideon's mood. "Nothing on my home surveillance system was of use. After the detective downloaded a copy, I watched it myself. My street is quiet, and a strange man tampering with a parked vehicle outside my house would have stood out. It's creepy to think he waited in her car until she left."

Gideon tapped a few keys and read the screen. "My hope is that he was following her. But the footage from your house doesn't show anyone following her, though your street view wouldn't necessarily catch someone parked down the road and waiting. The surveillance system at the gas station didn't get a good glimpse of the guy. But it didn't show anyone climbing into the car while it was parked, and Penny went inside. We have footage of the man coming back and stealing her car, but it's hard to know if he had an accomplice who dropped him off and fled the scene before the attacker grabbed her, or if the attacker was inside the car already. Honestly, it could be either or both. He could have had an accomplice watching her, and the perpetrator was likely inside the vehicle for a while."

Trenton peered at Gideon's screen. "Doing what? Why wait?"

"I don't know. But if he knew her routine, then taking her after she left your house would make the most sense. No one would have missed her right away. If she hadn't shown up at your house, you would have called me. But if she worked, hung out at your house for date night, and then left, no one would know she was missing, possibly until Monday when she didn't show up for work."

"Then that would mean this creep has been watching her for a while."

"Likely." Gideon tapped a few more keys. "Spontaneous or convenient kidnappings are not unusual by any means. Sometimes people are just taken because they are in the wrong place at the wrong time. But often the kidnapper watches and waits. Some of them really get off on watching their target without their knowledge, knowing what is going to come. And knowing when the best time to strike is."

Trenton was quiet for a moment. "You'll find him."

Gideon's fist clenched. He wished he had the faith in himself that he heard in Trenton's voice. But Gideon would do whatever was necessary to find him and bring him in.

Chapter Six

Two days later, they still had nothing. Gideon was frustrated but knew the detective working the case was doing his best. But it was like the man had appeared out of thin air and disappeared the same way. The analysts had managed to find enough footage to track Penny and her attacker until Penny had dodged into the alleyways and disappeared. Their perp then followed a similar path, and that's where the cameras lost him, too. The man kept his hat on, and the screen captures of his face were not much better than the glimpse Penny had gotten of him.

But right now, Gideon was more worried about Penny. She was getting antsy, and he wasn't sure she was going to tolerate being cooped up much longer. Clara seemed to be content to work from the Camhion's home and didn't seem inclined to leave. Between work and the party, Victoria was also happy to stay home and finalize her plans for the fundraiser.

But Penny was another story. She, too, had opted to work from the house, and no doubt being cooped up was frustrating for her. Nash had called and told him he had better get over there and get Penny out of the house before she took it upon herself to leave. So Gideon had rolled out of bed, showered, shaved, and pulled on one of his new outfits. In habit, he pulled up his hair and grabbed his old, battered leather jacket before grabbing his keys and heading to the Camhion mansion. He glanced at his motorcycle longingly but went for the car.

The drive was a quiet one, with morning traffic already subsiding. Gideon knocked on the front door. The family had told him dozens of times he didn't have to knock, but he had never been comfortable using his key and coming in.

It was a disheveled Penny who answered the door. Thankfully, she looked through the window before opening the door, and Gideon was glad she was observing the protocols he had given.

"Hi. What are you doing here?" Penny scooped her hair back and wiped the dust from her forehead. A move that Gideon found incredibly sexy, especially when the hem of her t-shirt rode up and exposed her belly button.

"I'm here to escort you wherever you'd like to go."

Penny tilted her head. "Did Nash send you?"

Gideon declined to answer the question, knowing she wouldn't like the answer. "Why don't you grab your stuff, and we can spend the day outside?"

Penny didn't have to be asked twice. "Let me take a quick shower, and I'll be ready to go. Mom and Dad are in the dining room."

Gideon peeled off his jacket and put it in the hall closet. Victoria was a stickler for neatness and making oneself comfortable. She didn't believe in having staff live in the house, so often there was no one else around. Today he had noticed some discreet security watching the house. He had recognized the man in the car as one of the men he had recommended to the family.

"Morning." Gideon leaned into the dining room. Victoria looked as disheveled as Penny had.

Victoria gave him a bright smile. "Gideon. We weren't expecting you."

"I'm here to take Penny out."

Victoria's smile got wider. "Thank goodness. She has been helping clean, but it hasn't been helping keep her mind off being stuck here. She was never one to sit still."

Gideon stayed in the doorway. "Nash sent me, but don't tell Penny. He said it was getting critical."

Eldridge laughed. "It is. Cleaning is Penny's least favorite thing to do. She hires people to clean her house. She says it's because she works too much. But she just hates doing it. So the fact that she's been helping clean goes to show you it's getting to the critical phase."

Gideon figured Penny would be a while, so he grabbed a rag and the wood cleaner and went to work. He still remembered when he'd first seen Victoria cleaning her own home. It had been such an incongruous sight that he'd stared. Victoria had noticed and asked him what was wrong. Not thinking, he'd dumbly told the truth. She had shaken her finger at him and said that money was no excuse for laziness. She said every person should be able to take care of themselves. She said everyone should know how to cook, clean, pay bills, and use proper etiquette on the phone. He figured he was good for three; his cooking skills were not great. And now, as an adult, he knew his phone etiquette was fine, but he hadn't known what that really meant at the time. And it was at that moment that he'd learned to relax around Victoria. As much as he'd grown to love her like a mother, she had always seemed above him. Seeing her wash dishes and scrub floors made him realize that she was the same as everyone else. And because of her, he'd learned to cook.

Penny entered the dining room and laughed as Gideon polished the side table. "Mom roped you in, I see."

Gideon turned and stopped in his tracks. Penny had her hair up in a twist that left soft tendrils down her neck, had dusted some light makeup on, and wore a form-fitting wool dress with a deep neckline and a belt cinched at her waist. She looked painfully beautiful to him.

Thankfully, Penny seemed oblivious to his stare. She took the rag and cleaner from him. She gave him a once over. "I see Nash took you shopping."

Gideon gave her a self-conscious nod. "Too much?"

Penny gave him a soft smile. "No. Perfect. You look great. You'll be the best-dressed detective in the precinct."

Gideon relaxed. "So Nash said."

Penny took his hand and waved her parents goodbye. "We'll be back later. Have fun."

"You, too, dear. And Gideon, don't let Penny boss you around." Victoria waved them off.

Gideon grabbed his jacket and Penny's from the closet. He helped her into it. "Where to?"

Penny locked the front door behind them after Gideon had taken a look around and made sure it was clear. She then gave him a mischievous grin. "Cantwell."

Gideon held the car door open. "Didn't Nash forbid you to go?"

Penny smoothed her skirt and slid expertly into the seat. "He did. But if you bring me, then he can't complain. You did say you would take me anywhere I wanted to go."

"I don't think that's what Nash had in mind."

"Ha. He did send you. I knew it. He can't mind his own business."

Gideon realized what he'd said. "He cares."

Penny slumped in her seat. "I know he does. But you have enough to worry about without adding me to your worries. And you're supposed to be on vacation. We don't have to go. I can help Mom clean the house. She's so anxious after what happened to me; she's been cleaning nonstop."

Gideon's voice dropped low. "I wouldn't be here if I didn't want to be."

Penny opened her mouth, probably to argue with him, but he was glad when she didn't. He put the car into drive and headed toward downtown.

Gideon listened to Penny's idle chatter as he drove. He had never been good at small talk, so he usually kept quiet. But it didn't really matter what Penny said; he enjoyed listening to her and her enthusiasm for whatever topic she came up with.

Forty minutes later, he parked in the small lot next to the unimpressive office building.

Penny wrinkled her nose. "This is where Cantwell's offices are? It's a dump."

Gideon silently agreed with her. On the outside, the building wasn't inviting. The brick was crumbling in spots, most of the windows were painted shut, though Gideon had fixed the windows in Cantwell's office, and the surrounding area had seen better days.

Gideon took Penny's arm and led her inside. "I don't take the elevator."

Penny stuck her foot out, relief in her voice. "Sneakers. We can take the stairs."

Gideon's gaze dropped to her feet. Startled, he realized he hadn't noticed she was wearing her pink, sparkly sneakers again. He'd been too busy admiring the rest of her.

Penny was puffing a little by the time they hit the top floor. "You left out the part where the office was on the fifth floor. I think I need to spend more time on the stair stepper at the gym."

Gideon stopped outside Cantwell's door. "I'm sorry. I wasn't thinking."

"It's fine. Given what the outside looks like, there is no way I was getting inside the elevator version of this building."

Relieved, Gideon opened the door. "Probably not what you were expecting."

Penny took in the room. There was a small table off to the side with a coffee pot, supplies, and snacks. There was a large drafting table, two computer stations, and a room off to the side. "It's not very big. Not Nash's normal style."

Gideon knew what she meant. Nash usually opted for opulence, if for no other reason than it was expected of him. Yet another reason for the prince moniker. "Since we all invested in this, and everyone kicked in equal amounts, this is all we can afford. It's just the four of us and Delilah."

At the sound of her name, Lilah rose. "Hey. You have to

be Penny."

The tall redhead walked with a slight limp as she made her way over. She held out a slim, delicate hand. "I'm Delilah, or Lilah. I think Isaac and Gideon are the only ones who use my full name."

Penny took her hand and shook it. "Penelope, or Penny. I think Gideon might be the only one to use my full name, except maybe my mother."

Lilah laughed. "Same. What brings you by?"

Penny waved her hand over the space. "I've been dying to see it, but Nash forbade me to come. So I used Gideon to get me in."

Lilah looked around. "It's not much. But this is the best job I've had. I'm the resident computer geek and graphic artist."

Gideon pointed to the portraits of the quartet on the wall. "Artist, period."

Penny looked where Gideon was pointing. Enthralled by what looked like paintings, Penny stepped over to get a closer look. "You did these?"

Lilah tucked her hands behind her. "Trenton took the pictures, and I drew them on paper until I got them right. Then I scanned them into the computer."

"These are amazing. They hardly look like they were computer generated."

Gideon stepped behind Penny. Trenton had decided each of the four characters in the video game needed to resemble them. So Trenton had spent hours taking pictures of them. Delilah had taken her favorites and converted them to drawings that she then translated into art on her computer. She had taken liberties with the clothing and backgrounds to fit the game's story. The development version of their game now had these likenesses in it.

Lilah went over to the large storyboard and moved it out of the way. "Now, these are better."

The portraits of four women, all facing away from the viewer, were framed and hung. These looked to be drawn and colored in with pencils. "You did these?"

Lilah pointed at Gideon. "I wish. Gideon drew these."

Penny drew closer. "I should have realized. Trenton's tattoo."

That piqued Lilah's interest. "Trenton has a tattoo?"

Penny traced a finger down the lines of the first picture. The woman was a blonde, her golden tresses slightly wavy, and her face in slight profile. "These are beautiful. Who are they?"

When Gideon remained silent, Lilah spoke. "They're the women in the game that Gideon, Trenton, Isaac, and Nash have to rescue."

Gideon spoke. "That's not their names."

Penny glanced at Gideon. He looked embarrassed. "Gideon drew Trenton's tattoo. I should have recognized the artist."

Gideon cleared his throat. "No reason to. It was just one tattoo."

"I'll have to for sure ask Trenton to see it."

Penny gave Lilah a facetious look. "The chest it's on isn't half bad, either."

Lilah grinned. "I like you. Feel free to come visit anytime."

Gideon's heart sank at Penny's comment about Trenton, but Nash interrupted before he could say anything stupid.

"Please don't." Nash popped out of the room to the side.

Penny started. "Hi, big brother."

Nash folded his arms over his chest. "Sister. What are you doing here? We're not open for business yet."

"It's your fault. You shouldn't have made Gideon come get me."

"I didn't…"

Gideon interrupted Nash. "I do what I please. And it pleases me to come get you."

Silence filled the room. Penny managed to muster an "Oh."

Nash dropped his arms. "See. But that isn't really an answer. And Gideon is right; no one makes him do anything."

Lilah patted Gideon's shoulder. "He'd have made a great knight in shining armor."

Nash pointed at Lilah. "Speaking of armor, we need to go over your recent drawings. There isn't any armor. In fact, the clothes don't fit the story at all."

Lilah wrinkled her nose. "Trust me, they do. I'll show you why."

Nash waved Lilah ahead of him while giving his sister a dirty look. "Finish your tour. And don't come back."

Penny stuck her tongue out at him. "He's always grumpy whenever I ask him about this project."

"Not grumpy. Impatient, perhaps. Eager. He wants everything to be perfect. He's investing so much time into this."

Penny glanced around with a new set of eyes. "It's important. Probably more important than anything else he's ever done. You can see him in it. He never had this much passion for Camhion Enterprises, his brief modeling career, or the six months he spent on an oil rig."

Gideon remembered those six months well. It had been either the oil rig or the military. Nash had wanted to join the military, but his mother had been so stressed over it that he had opted not to enlist. When Nash had returned, some of the shadows that filled his eyes had lessened. Gideon wouldn't say Nash came back a changed man, but he had exorcised some of his demons.

Penny interrupted his thoughts. "These are beautiful. This first one sort of looks like me, don't you think? And the third one, it sort of looks like Lilah."

Gideon spoke before thinking. "I dreamed them."

That got Penny's attention. "Dreamed them?"

Gideon shuffled his feet. "Lilah was going to work on the women. But I had the most vivid dream after re-reading Isaac's book we based the game on. So I sketched them when I couldn't sleep anymore. I showed them to Lilah. She refused to finish her drawings. Said they were mine to do. So I finished them. She hasn't transferred them to the game yet. She said she's not ready. Whatever that means. She's a character."

Penny traced the hair of the third woman. "I like her. She's got a lot of energy. I don't suppose Nash is attracted to her?"

Gideon sputtered for a second. "Uh, not that I know of."

Penny glanced at the open door. "He hasn't dated much

since Maggie. Not seriously, anyway. He really loved her. I worry he won't love anyone else."

Gideon turned to the fourth woman. He knew deep down that she was for Nash. "Sometimes a person can only love one person. It's too consuming. But as much as he loved Maggie, it was a young man's love. He'll find someone. But he'll do it in his own time."

Penny's eyes narrowed at the picture Gideon was looking at. Nothing of the woman's face was visible. She had sandy, sun-bleached blonde hair, a slim figure, and Penny had a feeling she was quite lovely. This one was for Nash. "Which one is for Trenton and Isaac?"

Gideon cleared his throat. "The brunette is for Trenton. And the redhead is for Isaac."

Penny felt her gut tighten. That left the first blonde, the one that looked like her, for Gideon.

Gideon snapped out of his mood. "It's not real, Penny, but I'm glad you like them. That they make you believe the story."

Penny pointed to the first woman. "Does your character fall in love with her?"

Gideon nodded. "They all do. Knights, dragons, and damsels in distress. All the things you need for a fantasy novel."

Penny sighed. "It's so very romantic, isn't it? But aren't Isaac's books science fiction? He doesn't really do fantasy."

Gideon walked over to the shelf where four copies of the book were sitting. "You haven't read this one yet. This is the book the game is based on. Isaac, too, said he dreamed this. He wrote it last summer."

Penny eyed the cover. "I remember Nash mentioning Isaac's book but that he wasn't letting anyone read it. It was at the same time Nash said he was going to create a video game and start his own company. So Nash came up with the company, Isaac wrote the book, Trenton did the photos that Lilah drew, and you did the women. That's amazing."

Gideon handed her the book. "I'm sure no one will mind if you read it. Since you already saw some of the drawings."

Penny clutched the book to her chest. "I can't wait to read this. And I'm keeping it. No way am I giving back the advanced copy."

Gideon laughed. "I had a feeling you'd say that. You can consider it a gift from me. That's my copy."

"Thank you, Gideon. It's the best present you could give me."

If she only knew how much he wanted to give her. He shook the thought off and finished walking her around the office. He showed her the storyboards Trenton had put together with photographs he'd taken on his travels. Many of the pictures from his trips to Ireland had ended up on the boards. Gideon had faith that Delilah would capture the depth and color of Trenton's shots.

"This is really amazing." Penny continued to glance back at the portraits of the women.

Gideon saw where her gaze was and walked over and poked his head into Nash's office. "I'm going to go feed your sister. We'll get out of your hair."

Lilah rolled her chair to the doorway and leaned around Gideon. "It was nice to meet you, Penny."

"Same. Good luck with these four."

"Never been better. First job I've had where I don't get harassed by the men I work with. Gaming is a hard business, and women are not always welcome. These guys don't know any better."

Penny laughed at Lilah's salute as she slid back into the office. Lilah's voice echoed in the now-quiet room where she continued her arguments about the clothes.

"I think she'll win." Penny picked up her purse and followed Gideon from the room.

"Nash has it on good authority that she's the best. Since none of us know our way around a computer, except for maybe Nash to some degree, we knew we'd need help. Lilah doesn't get to invest, but she's getting a healthy paycheck, and she'll get credit when the game comes out."

Penny tucked her arm around Gideon's. "That's what I love about the four of you. You play fair."

Gideon nodded. "It's the only way to play."

Chapter Seven

Penny enjoyed the day she'd spent with Gideon. She realized they had never spent time together, just the two of them. After spending an hour at Cantwell, he'd taken her to lunch, and then he took her to the park where they simply enjoyed the weather. It was still cool out, but the breezes were starting to get warmer, and summer was only a couple of months away. The sun shone down on them, and they contentedly relaxed on the benches that were scattered throughout the park. Then he'd done something that seemed out of character for him. He'd taken her out for ice cream.

She'd never been to the small shop hidden at the end of the strip mall, but the ice cream was homemade, and the most delicious she'd ever had. The owner had smiled at Gideon, called him Officer Eginhard, gushed over his beautiful guest, and fixed them the flavor of the day. Penny had been tempted to tell the man it was now Detective Eginhard, but she refrained. He seemed intent on not telling anyone, and she didn't want to embarrass him. Though why his promotion was a sore point for him, she didn't know.

After the ice cream, he'd gotten a text. He didn't tell her what it was about, but if she had to guess, it was about her.

But she had been reluctant to question him, and it had been such a lovely day; she didn't want to spoil it. He'd dropped her off at her parents' house after that. He'd then invited her to hang out with his mother tomorrow if she'd like. She'd jumped at it.

So here she was, sitting on an uncomfortable lawn chair on another beautiful day, chatting with Miranda Eginhard and sipping sweet tea while watching Gideon mow his mother's lawn. And she was doing her best not to ogle him in front of his mother. But he'd gone into the house in another outfit Nash had picked out and emerged in a tight t-shirt and a pair of basketball shorts. She was sure she'd never seen him in a pair of sandals.

Penny took a sip of her drink. "You must be awfully proud of him."

Miranda turned to where Penny was looking. "I've always been proud of him, but yes, I'm very proud of him. He works so hard; it's wonderful that his boss recognizes all he's done. But it's scary, too. I think he wanted to be a cop since the day he found out your grandfather had been killed during the kidnapping. He changed that day. He wasn't a kid anymore."

Penny could empathize. "It was like that with Nash. One day he cleaned out his room and boxed up every toy, and model car and plane. Anything he deemed childish. My mom cried and took the boxes filled with the things he wanted to throw away and put them in the attic. I guess she hoped he'd want them back. But he never did."

Miranda leaned back in her chair and crossed her ankles. "Nash and Gideon are very alike. Both are driven. Both know the horrors that life can hold. And they both do what's right."

Penny glanced back at Gideon. "Nash would wince. Gideon would argue. But you're right."

They were quiet for a time, each in their own thoughts. Penny was startled when Miranda spoke. "You're not the only one watching him. Old Mrs. Tattersall watches him every time he's over. I think she cries when it gets cold, and Gideon won't be back to mow until next spring. The woman is old enough to be his great-grandmother, I think."

Penny blushed. "I was hoping you wouldn't notice."

"I'm his mother. Hard to miss. He likes you; you know."

Penny frowned. "We're friends."

Miranda sat back up in her seat and set her drink down. "That's not what I meant. Friends is good, though, to start. But at the rate he's going, I'll be an old lady before he gives me grandchildren, assuming he ever does."

Penny sighed. "I like him, too. But I wouldn't bet money on him and me. I think he sees me as a sister."

Miranda scoffed at that. "Trust me, dear, he does not think of you as his sister. Quite the opposite, if that's a thing. You've not taken your eyes off him since you arrived. And he watches you when you're not looking."

Penny slumped in her seat. "We hardly know each other when it comes right down to it. Yesterday was the first time we'd ever spent a day together just the two of us. And it was only because Nash asked him to take me out that he came."

"Don't you bet money on that, either." Miranda was quiet for a moment, then she took a deep breath. "You'll have to make the first move. He won't do it on his own. He respects your family too much to do anything that might hurt one of you."

The punch of lust that hit her in the gut when she thought about making that move had her turning her head away from Miranda so she couldn't see the thought that was likely plastered all over her face. She could very much imagine slinking up to Gideon, running her palms over that glorious chest of his, pressing her body against his, and kissing him the way she'd dreamed of kissing him. And in those dreams, it did not end with a kiss.

"Think about it, at least. He's shy."

Penny jerked her head. "Shy? Seriously?"

Miranda gave Penny a serious look. "When it comes to matters of the heart, yes, he is. His girlfriends follow the same sad pattern. Some woman sees him, lusts after him, and hooks up with him. The relationship lasts for a time, but when he isn't what their fantasies told them he was, they ditch him. He's not the bad boy they imagine him to be. He looks like a big, tough guy, and in some ways he is. He has to be in order to be effective in his job. But he is also intellectual, respects people's opinions, and listens to what others say. Like I said, he's shy. And he's sensitive. He'd be the first to deny it, of course, but it's there just the same."

Penny didn't like Miranda's descriptions of Gideon's former lovers. "I don't do hookups."

Miranda patted her hand, satisfied with her response. "I know. That's why I said you'll have to make the first move. You might make the first move, but it won't take long for Gideon to make his own. He never bothered with the others. But he will with you."

Penny covered her hot cheeks with her palms. "I can't believe we're talking about this."

"Hey, I was married and had two children. I remember many a time watching Gideon's father. Landon Eginhard was easy on the eyes, that's for sure. I had to make the first move with him, too. Gideon is a lot like his father, even though they didn't have much time together."

Penny shifted in her seat, giving the woman her full attention. "Your husband died young, didn't he?"

Miranda's eyes were wet when she looked over at Gideon. "He did. Gideon was so young. Iris even more so. Iris barely remembers him. But he loved all of us. The cancer hit fast and took him before we had even accepted his diagnosis was real. I was grateful it went quickly, once the cancer took over. But it devastated all of us. Gideon tried too hard to take his father's place. It worried me. I tried to tell him it wasn't his responsibility; it was mine to run the family. But his heart told him that he was now the man of the family, and it was his responsibility to look after me and his sister. He did an excellent job, too, if I say so myself. I know I've thanked your parents a hundred times for what they did for my son. And they have thanked me as many times for what my son did for theirs. It seemed like fate intervened that day and put those two boys together in the same place. Gideon never did say what he was doing out so late, but for the sake of your brother, I'm glad he was."

Penny wiped a tear from her cheek. "I have always felt guilty because of what happened to Gideon. But I wouldn't take it back for anything."

Miranda gave her a knowing look. "Is that why you hold back? Because you're glad your brother is alive at Gideon's expense? My son was hurt and permanently scarred. But none of us, especially Gideon, would wish your brother dead in return for that never happening to him. You need to let that go. It was not a choice either of them had. And it made both of them the men they are today."

Penny gave her a watery laugh. "We should chat more often."

Miranda gave Penny a soft smile. "Yes, we should. I'm going to go inside and start supper."

"I can help." Penny rose, picking up both glasses of tea.

"You know how to cook?"

Penny followed her in. "Yes. My mother is a firm believer in the fundamentals. Truth be told, I think she believes the old saying, the way to a man's heart is through his stomach. My father found any and every excuse to invite himself over for dinner when he was courting my mom. My mom would bake a dessert every time. Thankfully, my mom didn't realize he was the heir to the Camhion fortune. My mom would have bolted before she ever got to know him."

Miranda opened the fridge and took out the makings for homemade spaghetti and meatballs. "Your mom grew up in a wealthy family, didn't she? I'd think they'd be the perfect match. Seems to me they are."

Penny took the vegetables to wash them. "She did. And they are. My father adores her, and my mother still blushes when he compliments her. My father will still steal a kiss when he thinks no one is looking. But my mom's parents were vastly different from my father's. My father's family was close. Money was just something they had. It wasn't what defined them. For my mom's family, money and prestige was everything. My mother grew to hate it. She left home when she turned eighteen and got a job as a secretary. She refused to take money to go to college or for anything else. She took the clothes from her closet and left most of her other possessions behind. By then, she had met my father while she worked at a drive-in movie theater on the weekends. It took my dad two years to convince my mother to marry him. She wanted to prove she could live on her own. And then another two years to actually marry him after she met his parents. She called off the engagement the day she met his parents and realized who they were, but my father was very persistent."

Miranda took a couple of pans out and handed Penny a cutting board and knife. "Well, I'm very glad he was. I like your parents. I was intimidated by them when I met them, no doubt about it. But they are good people, and they put good out into the world."

Penny wiped away a fresh tear. "So do you."

The women dropped into silence and worked side by side to fix dinner. That is how Gideon found them half an hour later.

"That smells great. What did I do to deserve my favorite meal?"

Miranda scoffed. "Everything is your favorite meal."

Gideon went and looked in the pot. "It is when you cook it."

Penny held up the knife. "Hey, I get credit here, too."

Dark eyes turned to Penny. "So you do. Victoria's doing, no doubt."

Penny went back to the veggies. "You know Mom. You don't cook, then you don't eat. Nash was never particularly good at it, but Mom made him keep trying. It got to the point where, when it was his turn to cook, he'd cook the same thing every time."

Gideon took a seat at the kitchen table and relaxed. "Steak and a salad. He probably had red meat oozing from his pores."

Penny stopped and stared. "That was a joke."

Gideon thanked his mother as she set a glass of tea in front of him. "I've been known to make one now and again. Probably Trenton's influence."

"That's so sweet."

Gideon eyed Penny. "Your eyes are red."

Penny glanced at Miranda, who chuckled under her breath. "Onions. You know, for the spaghetti."

The onion sat uncut on the counter, which Penny didn't realize until after she said it. She saw the moment Gideon noticed it on the counter. He stayed silent.

Penny and Miranda finished cooking the meal while Gideon set the table. Conversation was steady as they ate, mostly between Penny and Miranda. But Gideon would interject from time to time.

Dinner was just finished when Iris came into the kitchen. She leaned down and kissed her mother and then her brother on the cheek. "Mom said you two were stopping over for dinner today. I wanted to say hi."

Penny stood and gave Iris a hug. Iris was a few years

younger than Gideon, and Penny hadn't really gotten to know her until she had been a bit older. It never failed to amaze Penny how beautiful Iris was. She was only a little over five feet, had curves Penny was envious of, had black hair down to her waist, and the same brown/black eyes as Gideon's. She also had his serious temperament.

Iris went and fixed herself a plate. "Mom told me what happened. How are you doing?"

Penny assured her that she was fine. "Your brother came to the rescue."

Iris's gaze softened when she looked at her brother. "He's really good at that."

Gideon started clearing the table. "How was school?"

Iris swallowed her bite before talking. "Exams. I don't know what possessed me to go back to school to get my nurse practitioner's license. The schoolwork has been brutal. But only a couple more weeks, and then I can take the exam to get my license."

Miranda gazed back and forth between both her children, but her eyes landed on Iris. "We are so proud of you. Though, I wish you would quit that job already. It's dangerous."

Gideon handed Iris a glass of sweet tea. "So I've told her a hundred times. I don't enjoy seeing my sister when I go to the ER with a gunshot or stabbing victim."

Iris shrugged. "It's the best place to get experience in the city. If I can handle the graveyard shift uptown, then I can handle anything. But I really hope to get a job at a clinic in the next six months. Until then, pray for me."

Penny could only be envious of her. "I think it's great.

You get to save a small part of the world. Just like Gideon."

Gideon dropped back into his chair. "So Iris tells me."

Iris's dark eyes went from Gideon to Penny. Penny flushed under Iris's intense stare.

"So how long has this been going on?"

Gideon growled. "Mind your own."

Iris's dark brow rose at that. "Not on your life."

Penny defused the fight brother and sister looked like they were about to have. "Gideon is taking pity on me and getting me out of the house while we try to find the guy who attacked me."

Iris pointed her fork at Gideon. "If Gideon can't, then no one can. It's his sixth sense."

Gideon had enough. "Eat your dinner, Iris."

Iris gave him a mischievous salute. "Yes, sir."

* * *

Two hours later, Penny buckled her seat belt. It was dusk, and Penny was so full she thought she'd burst. "It was nice seeing your mom and Iris. I haven't seen Iris in a while."

"She's been buried in her studies between shifts. Mom worries about her, so Iris stops by to show her she's fine. Mom then feeds her, and Iris loves every minute of it."

Penny patted her stomach. "No, kidding. Your mom can cook."

Gideon flipped the turn signal. "I know. Best part of my childhood was dinner."

Penny stared out at the darkening sky. "I can see why.

Must have been hard after your dad died. Your mom told me a little about it. I didn't know he died of cancer."

Gideon gave her a brief glance before turning his eyes back to the road. "I guess it's not something I talk about. It was hard on all of us. But my mom was devastated. I remember how hard she cried when she had to sell the house and we moved into an apartment on the outskirts of town. I never want to see her grieve like that again. She still misses him. But it got easier as the years passed. She even occasionally has dinner with a man she met at work. She says they're just friends, but it's nice that she has a companion."

"I think that's nice. It must be lonely sometimes now that Iris has moved out on her own."

Gideon nodded. "But I think they were both ready."

Penny understood that. She loved her mother, but it had been past time for her to have her own place. She had opted for a downtown apartment for a time, so she'd be close to work. When she bought her house, she finally felt like she'd set down some roots and was ready to make a home.

Gideon pulled into her parents' driveway and killed the engine. "You and my mom had a cozy chat. What else did you talk about besides my dad?"

Penny was glad it was dark inside the car because she knew she was blushing. "Lots of stuff. Girl stuff, mostly."

"Girl stuff?"

Penny remembered what Miranda had said, and she felt a little burst of excitement in her belly. "Walk me to the door, and I'll show you."

Penny didn't wait for Gideon to open her door but

opened it herself and slid out.

"Show me?"   Gideon pocketed his keys, his eyes narrowing at her.

Penny waited until Gideon came around and she walked up to the front porch. She took one of Gideon's hands. "My dad used to sit in the parlor and wait for me to come home from my dates. He wasn't very discreet either. The boy who was with me would see him sitting with the newspaper, and the poor kid would clear his throat and bid me goodnight. Burst all my teenage longings to have my date kiss me goodnight."

"Penny…"

Penny didn't slide her hands up Gideon's chest, and she didn't press herself against him. He looked wary. But she wanted to make that first move. She braced one hand on his shoulder and stood on her tiptoes. She pressed her lips to his, lightly at first. He stood completely still, but she was determined. She gripped his other shoulder. When that didn't work, she pulled back. "Gideon, I swear if you don't kiss me back, I'll never speak to you again."

Penny saw Gideon swallow, saw his eyes darken, but she could also see he was very much in control. Figuring she had nothing to lose, she wrapped her arms around his neck, brought her body flush to his, and plastered her lips to his.

Penny was just about to give up in defeat when Gideon's hands came around her waist. He didn't grab at her or touch her anywhere else but her back. But his lips softened over hers, and she melted against him when he finally kissed her back. It wasn't necessarily a passionate kiss that led to more, but there was something inherently sweet about it, as if he were memorizing her mouth with his. And when Penny no longer had control of the kiss, and Gideon took control, she felt all of her tension fade away. He had made his move.

Penny lost track of time. Gideon didn't attempt to deepen the kiss, but he fully participated, and she felt more emotion pour through her than she imagined she could feel. She sighed when Gideon pulled back from her. And she felt his rough fingertip wipe away a small tear.

Penny hugged him for a moment, then let him go. "I should let you get home. You had a long day."

Gideon took a step back, his eyes uncertain on hers. "You okay?"

Penny wiped a second tear. "Sorry, onions again."

Gideon nodded at that. She could see he wanted to ask her what the tears were about, but she didn't have an answer to give him. So she stepped back and opened the door at her back. "Goodnight, Gideon."

"Goodnight, Penelope."

Penny slipped between the door and closed it behind her. She watched as Gideon hesitated for a moment, then pulled his keys from his pocket and left.

Well, she had made the move Miranda told her to make. She touched her lips and closed her eyes for a moment.

"Everything okay?" Victoria came into the hall.

Penny's eyes shot open. "Hi, Mom. I'm fine. I had a nice time at Mrs. Eginhard's house."

Victoria's eyes brightened. "How is she doing?"

"She's well. She sends her best. Iris does too."

Victoria took a step closer to her daughter. "You look

flushed. Are you sure you're okay?"

"I'm fine. Not sure about Gideon, though."

"Is he okay? Did you have a fight?"

Penny laughed. "No. I kissed him."

Victoria grinned. "It's past time. You've been dancing around him for years. How was it?"

Penny's mouth pinched. "I'm not sure it's appropriate to ask me if Gideon is a good kisser. And I have not been dancing around him."

"Penelope, I love you, but that is a huge fib. You have been dancing around him since you got back from college. Maybe before. He's an intense man, and it can take time to get used to him. But he has a big heart, and if you gave him the chance, he'd love and adore you forever."

"Mrs. Eginhard pretty much said the same thing. But he was always standoffish. It's only since my attack that he's been coming around. What if that is all it is? His sense of duty?"

Victoria tried to ease her fear. "Trust me, a mother knows. Especially one like Miranda who raised her children well."

Penny crossed to her mom and hugged her, seeking comfort. "I have real feelings for him. What if he doesn't?"

Victoria brushed her hair back from her forehead. "I think he's worth the risk to find out, don't you?"

Penny wiped the last of her tears. "He is. He won't know what hit him."

Victoria wrapped her arm around her daughter's waist and led her toward the stairs. "That's my girl."

Chapter Eight

Most people would assume Penny fit right in with this crowd. The blue silk dress fit her slim figure perfectly. Her silver high-heeled sandals added height. Her golden blonde hair was up in the perfect twist, with delicate silver combs keeping the locks in place. She wore minimal jewelry and minimal makeup, but she garnered much attention from both men and women.

But in all honesty, Penny hated parties. She liked to dress up when the occasion called for it, but she'd rather be in her sneakers and jeans, hanging out with friends, having pizza with Trenton, or having a girls' night with Clara and her mom, anything else but parties.

Clara was in her element mingling with guests, explaining the benefits of investing in the local neighborhood and youth programs, and charming everyone she came in contact with. Her mom enjoyed the planning of the parties but was relieved when they were over. But she, too, worked the room, explaining the benefits of investing in the community and in Camhion Enterprises.

Penny knew her role, and she played it well. She, too, mingled with guests, answered any of their questions, and rebuffed a few advances. She guessed Clara did the same, but with more grace than Penny did. Penny couldn't seem to drum up polite ways of saying no to men who she knew were more interested in her bank account, or her father's, than in getting to know her. Mostly she wanted to tell them where they could shove their feigned interest in her. But because she didn't want to cause a scene, she kept her comments more polite than she felt.

Penny glanced at the slim white gold wristwatch for the tenth time in as many minutes. Gideon had texted her that he was running late but would be there soon. Security had been beefed up, so she wasn't worried about intruders. But since the kiss two days ago, she'd done nothing but think about it and how she wanted to do it again. She had been anticipating seeing him today ever since.

"Relax, sis, he'll be here." Nash handed Penny a glass of champagne.

"That obvious, huh?"

Nash took a sip from his glass. "It's only because I know you so well. And Gideon was acting strange yesterday. Did something happen between you two?"

Penny was not going to discuss kissing Gideon with Nash the way she had with her mother. "No. We visited his mother the other day and had dinner."

"Mmm. If you say so." Nash changed the subject. "Not a bad turnout. Dad is not happy with all the people here, but Mom is ecstatic that she had such a good turnout."

What had started as a small real estate and land development company seventy years ago had become Camhion Enterprises. Three generations of Camhions built the empire that Eldridge now controlled. Penny knew her dad wished Nash would take a more active interest in the company, but also knew Nash's passions lay elsewhere.

Penny loved working with her father. Now that her dad was semi-retired, she and her team managed a lot of the day-to-day work, with her father stepping in when it came to meetings with the board and investors. Clara handled public relations, and she was very good at it. But Penny was now the face of the company. She spent a lot of her time working with different real estate agents, land developers, building commissioners, architects, and builders. She especially loved meeting the tenants and shop owners who occupied Camhion properties. It was the people who invested their time and energy into Camhion that were the heart and soul of Camhion, and her father had taught her that happy tenants and happy property owners were at the core of what Camhion stood for.

Nash and Penny chatted a bit longer, as well as greeting people as they passed by. Penny was getting to the point where she was going to text Gideon to see where he was when he came through the front door. She must have made some sort of sound because Nash turned as she did, but she couldn't be sure because she was too busy staring at Gideon. The charcoal suit he wore fit him everywhere a suit should fit. The tie he wore bore a subtle pattern, but she couldn't remember ever seeing him in one. The gray-blue shirt under the jacket contrasted with the deep brown color of his eyes. His dark hair was parted to the side, the slight waves of his thick hair reaching his shoulders.

Nash slipped the glass out of his sister's hand. "I think that was the exact reaction he was hoping for. Why don't you go say hello to your date?"

Penny forgot a moment the ruse. Then she snapped out of her daze. "Yes, my date."

Penny lifted a hand so Gideon could see her in the crowd, but his gaze was already on her. She wove her way through the crowd. She stopped in front of him, lifted onto her toes, and kissed his cheek. "I was getting worried."

"Sorry. I was at the precinct."

Penny heard the word "precinct," and some of her joy faded. "Anything new?"

Gideon slipped his arm around her waist and led her away from the crowd. "Maybe. Your car was found. There were prints. Some belonged to a kid we know very well. I'm guessing your attacker stole your car, wiped it, and then left it where it would be a prime target for theft. The kid is at the station, telling the detective on your case he saw the man who abandoned the car. We were waiting for his lawyer; the kid wants to cut a deal in exchange for what he knows. Or claims to know."

"What do you think?"

Gideon shrugged. "Hard to say. Kid has a good eye for faces. Comes in handy in his line of work. If he weren't a criminal, he'd be a good cop. The detective will see if anything the kid has to say vibes with what you told us. But for the deal to work, he has to be telling the truth, and the evidence he says he has needs to be enough to convince the D.A. that he cooperated."

Penny shivered. "I guess it's a step in the right direction, anyway."

Gideon put a finger under her chin and turned her gaze his way. "It's how this works. We gather information, and then we verify it. It may turn out to be nothing, but any kind of movement is good."

Penny lifted a hand to the loose tendril of Gideon's hair. "I haven't told you that you look very nice tonight. Very handsome."

Gideon returned the compliment. "You look beautiful. But you always do."

"Gideon." Penny wanted him to kiss her, but knew that now was not the time or the place.

"I know. We'll talk about it later."

Penny was relieved that he wasn't going to pretend he didn't know what she meant. "Do you dance?"

Gideon shook his head. "I haven't in years. Your mother tried to teach me, but I have two left feet."

Penny doubted that very much. He was very coordinated and very much in control of his body. "I won't force you tonight, but I think it's time for a new teacher."

Gideon's heated gaze found Penny's. Penny shivered under that look. It was not a look she had seen aimed her way before. At least not from Gideon. That look had heat pooling in her belly. Penny blurted out her next question. "How about food?"

Gideon took a deep breath. "Food would be good."

Penny led him over to the massive buffet. "Anything a vegetarian could want."

Gideon took a couple of plates and handed one to her. There were numerous kinds of pasta, finger sandwiches, salads, fruit, and vegetables. The dessert table was overflowing. "Your mother outdid herself."

Penny smiled and heaped food on her plate. She was

suddenly starving.   "You wouldn't know; you haven't attended before. But yes, she did."

Gideon grunted at that and loaded up his own plate. Penny saw him smile at her when she bypassed the various cuts of beef, chicken, and seafood that were laid out. She grabbed a slice of cheesecake and led them over to a small table.

They were quiet for a time, enjoying the food on their overloaded plates. Penny broke the silence after taking a bite of the sinfully delicious cheesecake. "I have no idea what to say."

Gideon did. "I didn't want things to be awkward."

Penny pointed her fork at him. "It will only be awkward if you let it be."

Gideon took the fork from her that she was still waving at him. "Maybe we just need practice."

Penny was glad she didn't have food in her mouth; she might have choked on it in shock. She found her words. "Sounds like a good idea to me. How about right now?"

A waiter stopped and took their empty plates, but Penny barely noticed. She looked around and took his hand. She led him out to the gardens. Before she knew what happened, Gideon spun her on her heels and pulled her into his arms. His arms were steel bands around her, but she had no wish to escape him. With a soft whimper, she wrapped her arms around his neck and buried her fingers in his hair. Blindly she found Gideon's mouth with her own.

This time there was no softness, no hesitation. And Penny didn't have to threaten him to kiss her. He had her spun and backed up against the trellis before she could take a breath.

"Penny."

Penny heard the plea in his voice. Answering it, she raised her mouth back to his. She kissed him like she had been starving for a man's kiss. And perhaps she had been. For his kiss. She savored the feel of his hair under her fingers, the feel of his hard chest against her breasts, and the feel of his erection that he was trying to hide. Not caring who might come outside, she pressed herself against him, and she heard the low moan in his throat before he anchored her hips against his with a grip on her backside that she savored.

"Penny, we have to stop."

The rational part of her knew he was right. This wasn't the time or the place. But she had waited so long to feel him against her, to act on her desire for him, that she was reluctant to let him go for fear he'd pull away. "We could leave."

Before Gideon could answer, a woman's scream rent the air.

* * *

Gideon grabbed Penny and pulled her behind him. He reached under his jacket and pulled out the gun he was wearing. "Stay behind me."

He could feel Penny trembling behind him, but he had to block it out. He was no use to her unless he focused. Inside the dining area, a fire had broken out. It was spreading quickly. The security team grabbed the fire extinguishers that had been set out. Others grabbed the pitchers of water. Gideon's gaze went past them to the guests. He found Nash, who was urging his parents outside.

"Nash!" Gideon kept Penny close to his side as he made his way over. He grabbed a couple of men from the security team along the way.

"Gideon. Thank God. The room went up. I found my parents, but I don't see Clara anywhere."

Gideon pointed to the security men he'd grabbed. "Take them outside and don't let any of them out of your sight. Grab a couple of extra men. The Camhions are the target."

Nash shook his head. "We need to find Clara."

Gideon gently tugged Penny and handed her to her brother. "Get your parents and Penny outside. I'll find her."

Nash reluctantly did as Gideon asked. Gideon was grateful there was no further argument. But he wasn't surprised when Penny came back to him. "Be safe."

Gideon kissed her roughly. "I will. Go with Nash."

Penny nodded and went back to her brother, where her parents and the security team were urging them all to go outside.

Gideon hated leaving them, but he had a job to do. He could smell gasoline. The men and women from the security team had staunched most of the fire, but the room was filled with smoke. There was no telling if any other fires would be set and how many people could be hurt if he didn't find out who started the blaze.

Gideon kept his gun at his side, muzzle down. Party goers were still panicked, but they were now outside. Some of the guests at the other end of the house hadn't realized what had happened, but word had spread. The only people still inside that Gideon saw were security. But Gideon couldn't help but feel someone else was still in the house.

Gideon knew the security team would have already called the fire department and police. But Gideon grabbed his phone and dialed his captain.

"Captain Barnes."

"It's Gideon. Someone set a fire at the Camhion residence. I think it was a Molotov cocktail. I can smell gasoline, and the burn patterns are consistent. I need the lead detective to come out here. And I need to get the Camhion family safe. Right now, all are accounted for except Clara Brooks, the niece of Eldridge Camhion and an employee. I'm looking for her now, but I don't see her."

"I heard it come over the wire. Detective McQueen is on his way. I don't suppose I have to remind you that you are not investigating this."

"No, sir. I was Penny's date. I just happened to be here." Gideon lied through his teeth, keeping his eyes peeled for Clara.

Barnes's tone was sarcastic. "Sure. All right. Help secure the crime scene. Don't let anyone leave. You're in charge until McQueen gets there."

"Yes, sir." Gideon stuck his phone back in his jacket pocket when he heard the line go dead. He continued searching. Still nothing.

After half an hour of searching, there was still no sign of Clara. He made his way back to the Camhion family. He'd kept them in his peripheral vision when possible as he'd looked. He saw McQueen get out of his vehicle and wave him over. Gideon held a finger up at Nash and made his way over.

"Detective McQueen."

The older man scanned the crowd. "Anyone hurt that you're aware of?"

Gideon shook his head. "Right now, we have one person unaccounted for. No injuries that I'm aware of."

McQueen's eyes continued to take in the scene. "You told the captain Clara Brooks was missing. Take it you didn't find her. We'll need to get the guest list and start going over names. And we'll need to check it against everyone who is here. Unfortunately, it's likely the perp has already vanished."

Gideon knew that was the likely scenario, but he still felt that prickle on the back of his neck that told him the danger was not over. "I have a copy of that list. I sent it to the security team to vet."

"Good. And what were you doing here?" McQueen turned sharp eyes to Gideon. "I believe you are on vacation. I did hear rumors you're a close friend of the family."

Gideon retold his lie, though after the garden, it didn't feel like one. "I was Penelope Camhion's date. And yes, I'm a friend of the family. After Penny was assaulted, they've been taking extra precautions. And they felt better having me here."

Detective McQueen seemed satisfied with the answer. "This is a cluster. There must be a hundred people here. It would have been easy for the perp to snatch Clara if kidnapping any member of the Camhion clan was the goal."

Gideon knew the detective was aware of the letters. Eldridge would have kept Victoria close by. And he had kept Penny close to him. He knew Nash was keeping an eye on Clara, but with all the people and distractions, it would have been easy for Clara to disappear from his sight. And since Clara didn't particularly like Nash, it was likely she'd given him the slip without a second thought. With all the security, the family felt safe.

The police and crime scene investigators' work got underway, and the scene of the fire had been taped off. The detective had lined people up so he could check them off against the guest list. Gideon made his way back to the family.

"I'm sorry. There is no sign of Clara. The police are looking for her, and we have a call out on the wires to be on the lookout."

Victoria covered her mouth to muffle her soft cry. "Do you think someone took her?"

Gideon's eyes found Penny's. Tears were there, as was fear for her cousin. He looked back at Victoria. "I'm sorry, but it's a likely scenario. I doubt she would have left on her own."

Penny looked down at her phone. "We've been calling her, but there is no answer. She always has her cell phone."

Gideon knew there was already a trace on her phone. "Right now, the phone is off. If it comes back on, the police will know."

Eldridge held his wife as she wept. "Clara would not have shut it off. Someone must have her."

Gideon felt the sick feeling in his stomach and knew she

was taken. But he had to let the police in charge do their jobs. "Right now I need to worry about all of you. This person came right into your home and lit it on fire in the middle of a crowd of people. That's bold. Officers will be questioning everyone to see if they saw anything."

Nash scrubbed his hand through his hair. "And a perfect distraction. When the fire broke out, I was so busy looking for my parents that I lost track of Clara."

Eldridge tried for a positive tone. "We'll find her. The police are already looking for her. When a ransom demand is made, we'll pay whatever it takes to get her back."

Nash's voice was harsh, memories he tried to bury coming to the surface. "Like my kidnappers did?"

Penny hugged her brother. She had no comforting words, so she was silent. Gideon knew Nash knew better than anyone else here what Clara was going through. "There is no evidence that the same person who kidnapped Nash is the same person who tried to abduct Penny and grabbed Clara. Don't compare them. We need to look at this without any bias."

When no one said anything or argued with him, Gideon continued. "Eldridge, is there somewhere you can all go where no one can find you?"

Nash jumped on him. "Screw that, Eginhard. I'm not going anywhere. I'll be damned if we run from this guy."

Eldridge laid a hand on his son's shoulder. "You could stay at your office. No one but family knows about it. I can take Victoria and Penny to visit my mother. I doubt anyone would look for us there."

Penny's eyes filled. "I don't want to leave Nash. I could

go with him."

Nash turned tortured eyes to Gideon. "My parents should be safe. We can send a couple of men with them. But I think Penny should stay with you. I want you watching her."

Gideon shook his head. "You're not thinking straight. Penny will be safer if she goes. You, too."

Penny was looking at her parents. Gideon knew what she was thinking. She had been the original target, and when that didn't work, they grabbed Clara. He knew she wanted to be as far away from her parents as she could get to keep them safe. Gideon agreed it was highly unlikely the kidnappers would target Victoria and Eldridge, especially if they left town. If the goal was to torture them, it was working. Victoria was burrowed against her husband's chest. Nash had his arms wrapped around his waist; his solitary stance was one Gideon had seen many times when Nash was struggling with the demons of his past. And he knew there would be no budging him.

"All right. Victoria and Eldridge will visit Grandma Camhion. Nash will stay at the office, with guards outside the building. And Penny can stay with me."

Victoria sniffled and transferred herself to Gideon. She laid her head on his chest for a moment. Then she found her resolve and looked Gideon in the eyes. "Take care of my babies, Gideon. And take care of yourself. Don't do anything foolish. Promise me."

Gideon brushed a kiss on her brow. "I promise."

It was hours before the family was allowed back inside to pack up some clothes and essentials. The mood was somber, and when it came time to part, the family hugged each other until Gideon gently nudged them on their way.

Nash was the first to leave to head to his apartment to gather his things, two guards following him. Victoria and Eldridge already had a private car booked that would drive them to Baltimore. Guards would follow them and keep an eye out for anyone following them until they were a safe distance from D.C.

Gideon kept Penny at his side while the police continued to question the guests. He'd stopped in and chatted with Detective McQueen already, and he was aware of what the family had decided. The detective had looked relieved that the family was going into hiding while the search for Clara was underway.

"So now what?" Penny sagged against Gideon.

"Not much else we can do right now. Names will be run down on all the guests: the security team, the caterers, and anyone else who could be involved. Evidence has been gathered by the forensic team, as well as the arson investigator. Now we let them do their jobs and see if any of the evidence points to anyone."

Penny shivered. "I can't believe this is happening. And it doesn't seem right to leave Nash alone."

Gideon gently led her to his car. He did a thorough check of it before letting Penny get in. He buckled her seat belt when her hands were shaking too badly to fasten it. "It's okay, Penny. Nash won't be alone. I already texted Isaac and Trenton about what happened and to go stay with him. Anyone looking for Nash would look for him with one of us. But they won't find him."

Penny felt better knowing Nash wouldn't be alone. "Thank you for doing that. But won't people be looking for me with you?"

"It's possible but not likely. But my apartment is more secure than a hotel. Other than you sleeping on the cold floor of Cantwell with a bunch of snoring men, my apartment is the best option. I thought about sending you to my mom or Iris, but I can't risk it."

"Of course not. I would refuse to go."

Gideon drove down the darkened streets. The sky was pitch black. Rain clouds had come through, and a light rain was now falling. He kept his eyes on the road and checked to make sure no one was following them but kept his peripheral vision on Penny. She was huddled in her seat, his leather jacket from the back seat now wrapped around her like a blanket.

"What do you think they're doing to her?" Penny's voice held tears, and her voice trembled.

Gideon was not without sympathy, but he knew imagining the worst was not helpful. "Penny, don't do that. You need to stay positive that we'll find her. Just like we found Nash."

Penny's voice choked. "You found Nash, not the police. They looked but couldn't find him."

"Wrong place, right time. That's how I found him. Crimes have been solved on nothing more than that. But McQueen will splash her face all over the press and they'll keep looking until they find her. I'll keep looking until we find her. Back when Nash disappeared, the family tried to hush it up, and the public's focus stayed on your grandfather's murder. This time we'll use the press to our advantage."

Penny clutched the jacket closer. "She'll hate that, you know. She might be in charge of public relations, but she is a very private person."

Gideon couldn't offer any comfort, so he let Penny be with her thoughts.

When he pulled into the parking lot of his apartment building, all was clear. No headlights followed them, and no one was out and about this late. He glanced at Penny, who had fallen asleep in her seat. He knew the adrenaline crash would come. He hated to wake her, as he knew sleep would be hard to come by until Clara was found. But he couldn't carry her and her suitcase, and he wasn't about to leave her alone, not even to his apartment and back.

Gideon grabbed her suitcase from the trunk and went around the car. He opened the door and nudged Penny awake. "Come on, sweetheart. We're here."

Penny jolted awake. "I can't believe I did that."

Gideon helped her from the car and locked it behind them. The lot was empty of people and silent. The heels of Penny's sandals on the pavement were the only sound as he led them inside. He was on the fourth floor and knew she was not up to a trek up the stairs tonight. She stayed silent on the elevator ride up. He unlocked the door and urged a suddenly reluctant Penny inside.

Gideon guided her with a touch of his hand. "It's not much. But it's clean and I went shopping this week, so we won't starve."

Penny couldn't hide her curiosity. "I guess this is what I

imagined. A place to crash after work. You strike me as a minimalist."

Gideon carried the suitcase into his bedroom. "You'll have to sleep in here. It's the only private space in the apartment. I'll sleep out here. And don't argue."

Penny closed her mouth. "I didn't think about there being only one bedroom."

Gideon didn't suppose she had. She had grown up in a home that had bedrooms to spare. Gideon didn't need an extra room, so he hadn't bothered to rent a larger apartment. "I'll go change the sheets and let you settle in. Are you hungry? Thirsty?"

Penny clutched her stomach. "No. I'm not sure what is in there will stay down. I'm not feeling well."

Gideon went to the bathroom and found something he hoped would help soothe her stomach. She took it without a word. She then watched him from the doorway while he stripped the bed and put fresh sheets and pillowcases on it. "There is a TV on the dresser if you want to watch it. Not much to watch, other than free stuff. But it can help you sleep if you'd like."

"I feel exhausted, but I don't know if I'll sleep again."

Gideon set her suitcase next to the bed. "You should try. Not sleeping isn't going to do anyone, including yourself, any good. I should know."

Penny touched his shoulder. "You see stuff like this every day. How do you sleep?"

Gideon eased her into a sitting position on the bed. "I think about the good things. I think about things that I can control. And I remember all the people that I love and who love me. Then I sleep, get up the next day, and do my best to fix what's wrong with the world around me."

Penny turned to him, hugged him to her, and tucked her cheek to his chest. "That's nice. My family loves me, and I love them. Kissing you tonight was a very good thing. And I can't control what is happening to Clara, but I can rest and get up in the morning and do my best to help you find out who did this."

Gideon kissed the top of her head. He wondered what she would say if he told her she could add him to the list of people who love her. Instead, he held her until she pulled away. "Get some sleep. I'll be right out there."

He grabbed a spare pillow and blanket from the closet and grabbed a pair of jogging pants and a t-shirt. It was the best he could do for pajamas. "Good night, Penelope."

"Good night, Gideon."

Gideon shut the door behind him. He knew he'd drive himself crazy if he stood there any longer, trying to hear the sounds of her undressing. So he did what he did each night. He went to his desk. He opened the drawer and looked at the file but didn't pull it out. Detective McQueen would have people chasing down the lead that came in on Penny's car. He hoped the forensic team would find a fingerprint, fiber, or hair; anything that the attacker might have missed. Unfortunately, there would also be evidence from the kid who stole the car inside it now. The scene was badly contaminated, but Gideon could hope.

And that was his biggest problem. Hope. What was he doing with Penny? He'd wanted her to the point of no return at the party. When she suggested they leave, he would have dragged her to his car himself. He wasn't even sure he could have made it to his apartment or her house before he ravished her. And that is exactly what he would have done. And she would have let him. But when it was over, would it be enough? Once desire was satiated, would she still want him?

Gideon wasn't used to feeling insecure when it came to women. But Penny wasn't just any woman; she was the woman he wanted forever. His body still ached for her; he wanted to just accept whatever she wanted to offer him. But if it wasn't all of her, he wasn't sure he'd survive the aftermath.

Chapter Nine

Dim sunlight was filtering through the blinds when Penny woke. She'd taken Gideon's advice and tried her best to think of good things. She thought how grateful she was that her mom and dad were away. She was grateful that Isaac and Trenton were with Nash. They would keep him balanced. And they would make sure he didn't do anything stupid. She had seen the memories on his face yesterday when Gideon said Clara was missing. He never spoke to her about what happened the three days he had been missing. He had barely spoken a word when he returned home from the hospital. There had been a new level of stillness inside him. It was as if he were to move or speak, he would wake up from the dream and find himself back with his captor. To this day, their parents still worried about him. And when Nash's fiancée died, she feared he wouldn't make it. He had been at his breaking point. But his friends had pulled him back from the brink, especially Gideon.

But first and foremost, her thoughts were on Gideon. She wasn't sure what to do about her feelings for him. Should she blurt it out? Should she show him? And if she did, would he get the message? She had a feeling Gideon could be a bit dense when it came to matters of the heart.

How he didn't already know she was in love with him was beyond her. She wasn't one to indulge in random affairs, but she wanted to throw herself wholeheartedly into one with him. She was telling the truth when she told Miranda they didn't know each other well. But she knew enough, and it was enough for her.

Penny reluctantly rolled out of Gideon's bed, knowing sleep would not be returning. But given the circumstances, she was glad she had slept at all. No doubt Gideon's presence in the next room had helped. She looked at the blue silk dress draped over a chair he kept in the corner of the room. She'd had such high hopes last night when she'd donned the dress. She had hoped Gideon would find her beautiful in it. Now it sat, wrinkled and smelling a little of smoke, and a terrible reminder of the night. She wanted nothing more than to toss it in the trash.

Instead, Penny got dressed and grabbed her phone. There were no messages, though she wasn't surprised. Part of her had hoped Clara would text and that the whole ordeal had been a mistake. Instead, Penny first texted Trenton to see how Nash had fared through the night. Trenton's response was what she expected. He hadn't slept, but he wasn't alone, nor would he be. Penny then texted Nash to tell him she loved him and that she and Gideon were safe. A heart emoji was his response, which was more than she had expected.

Penny left the bedroom. Gideon was still asleep on the couch. Thankfully, his couch was oversized, and it held his length. The couch took up most of the room, and he looked comfortable. Somehow, she didn't doubt he fell asleep there sometimes, likely after a long day or even days of working.

She quietly made her way to the bathroom. She grimaced when she looked in the mirror. Her makeup was smeared, and her mascara had run down her cheeks from all the tears. Gideon hadn't said a word but had simply sent her to bed. Instead of just washing her face, she stripped and used the shower. There was both shampoo and conditioner in the shower, so she helped herself to both. The bar of soap had a very masculine scent, but it was all he had. But the scent was one she knew, one that lingered on Gideon's skin.

When she emerged from the bathroom, Gideon was in his compact kitchen making coffee. The apartment had just three rooms, with the living room and kitchen in one space. He had a battered desk off to the side and no kitchen table. She imagined he ate at his desk, poring over whatever he was working on, or at the coffee table in front of the TV.

Gideon poured two cups and handed one to her as she came over. "I don't have cream, but I have sugar."

Penny took a sip and shuddered at the bitter taste. "Sugar, please."

Gideon took out a container and spoon and let her doctor it herself. "How did you sleep?"

Penny took another sip, this time enjoying it. "Better than I thought. Your trick helped."

Gideon took a swallow of his coffee, no sugar. "I'm glad. Until we hear something, it's going to be exhausting. It's hard to say what the kidnapper's goal is until we hear from him. Or them. Detective McQueen called and got in touch with Clara's father. He is understandably distraught. He spent the night at the precinct, waiting to see if there was any word."

Penny's eyes widened. "They found Hayden Brooks?"

Gideon set his coffee cup down after draining the last of it. "Why is that surprising? I know Clara's mother passed away years ago, but her father wasn't hard to find."

Penny realized Gideon didn't know the story of how Clara had come to work for Camhion. "Can I get a refill? And can we sit?"

Gideon obliged and carried the cups to the couch. "So what don't I know?"

"Detective McQueen, too. Hayden disappeared over ten years ago. Twelve, I think. He had made several bad investment deals. He and my dad are cousins through marriage. There is no blood relation between the Brooks family and the Camhions. Hayden tried to prove he was smarter than my dad, and my grandfather, too. But he didn't have the same people skills, and people didn't particularly like him. So Hayden started throwing the Camhion name around, as if he had the business's backing. Major real estate deals fell apart, and Hayden disappeared with the investors' money. Charges were never formally filed; there wasn't enough evidence. It was deemed the deals simply failed, and the investment money was gone. But my father didn't believe that. He had a private detective dig into it. Turns out the Brooks' fortune was gone. The inheritance left for Clara after the death of her mother was gone, too."

"I guess it is not hard to guess what happened. Your father didn't have the heart to turn over what he'd discovered. Instead, he kept what he found to himself and gave Clara a job."

Penny cupped the hot coffee in her hands, staring at the dark brew. "Pretty much. As far as I know, Clara hasn't seen her father since he disappeared. But maybe she has and didn't mention it. No doubt my father would not be pleased if he knew Hayden was back in Clara's life."

Gideon rose and pulled a notebook out of his desk. Penny watched as he started jotting some notes down. Curious, she tried to take a peek, but Gideon kept the pad to where she couldn't see. "Like I said, Clara is a very private person. It's possible she has been in contact with her father and didn't tell anyone. Hayden Brooks would be ostracized if he were to start showing up. But because the family stood beside Clara in the aftermath, it was accepted that she had nothing to do with it. She would have been too young anyway."

Gideon jotted a few more things down. "Clara is your age, isn't she?"

"About. She is a year younger. What are you writing?"

Gideon closed the notepad. "I'd like to know more about Hayden. McQueen is probably already running a thorough check on him. But I can see if he has any criminal charges against him."

Penny's brows furrowed. "You think he could be behind this?"

"It's as likely a scenario as any. Given what you've said, he doesn't sound like a stand-up guy. And if Clara is a year younger, she would only have been seventeen when Hayden took off. It was nice that your parents took her in."

Penny shrugged, and her eyes started to water. "She's family."

Gideon sat stone still next to her. "The Camhions are generous that way."

Penny wiped her eyes. "Family, you mean? Of course, we are. It's what families do."

Gideon knew from experience that it was often not the case. But saying so wasn't helpful. "I should go take a shower. We have a lot to do. It will be easier if I go to the precinct."

Penny stared at his back in confusion. Yesterday he had kissed her like he could swallow her whole. This morning, he was back to being standoffish. She tried to shut out the hurt. "I'm ready when you are."

Gideon put his cup in the sink and headed to the bathroom.

Penny dropped her head into her arms, struggling to stem the tears.

* * *

Gideon felt like an ass but had to get away from her. Her hair was damp and loose. The jeans she wore lovingly hugged her legs and butt. Sitting next to her on the couch, smelling his soap on her skin, he had to muster all the willpower he had to not take her in his arms and kiss her. Now was not the time for any discussions about their future. And in the cold light of the rainy morning, he knew he needed to step back and give her the room she needed to come to grips with what was happening to her family.

Isaac had texted him that Nash had had a rough night and that Trenton had downplayed it for Penny. The reminder of Penny and Trenton's relationship had put a damper on his mood. He still wasn't convinced there was nothing more to their relationship than friendship. Gideon, too, needed to step back and think the situation through.

The ride to the precinct was a short one, and a quiet one. Both of them were lost in their thoughts. Gideon bet Penny's thoughts were on Clara. And after Clara, her brother. Gideon prayed Clara was still alive. He thought a ransom call would have come through by now, but so far nothing. The police had traces on all of the family's phones. It was uncertain who the kidnapper might contact. As the head of the family, the likely person was Eldridge.

Gideon unconsciously took Penny's hand as he helped her from the car and led her into the building. Keeping her close to him, he went to Detective McQueen's desk. The older man was there, glasses perched on his nose while he watched the security footage from last night's party.

The detective didn't look up. "Figured you'd show up, Detective Eginhard. I don't have anything new."

Gideon cringed a bit at the new title. That would take some getting used to. "I want to help. Penny, here, knows a bit about Hayden Brooks's history with the Camhion family."

McQueen paused the footage. "Please have a seat, Ms. Camhion."

"Penny, please. Gideon mentioned you were able to get ahold of Hayden Brooks. I was surprised because the family hasn't heard from him in years."

McQueen digested that. "There were rumors about fraud many years ago."

Penny nodded. "Gideon said you would be running a check on him. There was, but he was never charged. But my father had proof Hayden ran off with the investors' money on the land deals that supposedly fell through. My father paid in full all the money Hayden stole. We all assumed Hayden wouldn't show up again after he disappeared. Ever."

McQueen typed on his computer but had the screen turned so she couldn't see what he was typing. "I have it here; he has been back in town for more than two years. Town over, to be exact. He has been working as a real estate agent. Doing well for himself, as far as I can tell. Not Camhion well, but well by anyone else's standards."

Penny's displeasure at the insinuation was clear in her voice. "Be that as it may, it is news to us he's back. Did Clara know?"

McQueen's brow rose at her icy tone but didn't take the bait. "Mr. Brooks says yes. He claims they have been slowly building back their relationship. He also says Clara has forgiven him for what he did. A really touching story to hear him tell it. He's been vacillating between tears and anger since he got here. He's in an interview room. Refuses to leave."

Penny wrapped her arms around her waist. "Can I see him?"

McQueen locked his screen. "That would be up to him. He's here voluntarily. Same as you. I'll go check."

Gideon leaned against the desk as they waited. "What

are you thinking?"

She leaned into him. "Nash always teases me. You know, a penny for your thoughts?"

That elicited a smile. "Okay, a penny for your thoughts, Penny?"

"It's possible he's sorry and really has been rebuilding a relationship with Clara. Before all this happened, I liked Hayden. He was funny and would tell funny stories. He would bring small gifts, like candy and trinkets, when he brought Clara over to play. He and my dad were friends. When this came out, my dad was crushed that Hayden would betray the family this way. Seemed so out of character."

Gideon had heard that more times than he could count from family members of people who had been arrested for serious crimes. "Charm can hide a multitude of sins."

Penny glanced at him. "Is that why you don't bother?"

Gideon was startled. "To be charming?"

Penny pulled away and crossed her arms over her chest. "You didn't kiss me this morning. You didn't try to comfort me when I was crying. And no, charm is not your strong suit, but you seem to be good at being cross. I guess we're back to where we started."

Before he could respond to the accusation, not that it wasn't true, McQueen waved them over. "Interview room two. Cameras are on; he is aware. We're investigating an abduction. Nothing is out of bounds."

Gideon gave McQueen a curt nod. "Got it."

He took Penny's hand again and led her through the maze of hallways. He gestured to her to precede him. His first look at Hayden Brooks wasn't impressive. The man's hair was mostly gray. He was probably Eldridge's height but was much thinner. The hollowness of his cheeks was pronounced, and he didn't look like a well man.

"Hayden." Penny stood instead of taking a seat.

"Penny. It's good to see you. I was surprised when Detective McQueen said you'd like to see me. Where is the rest of the family?"

Gideon stopped her before she could speak. "Away. For now. Clara wasn't the only target."

The man's eyes were razor-sharp, a contrast to the rest of him. His sharp gaze turned to Gideon. "The detective told me someone tried to kidnap Penny first. I don't know who would do something like that. Especially after what happened to Nash; it seems incomprehensible."

Gideon pulled out a chair and sat. He found people responded to him better when he didn't loom over them. "Nash's kidnapping?"

"I was at the house when it happened. Eldridge swore me to secrecy. He didn't want his son to suffer any more than he already had. I was happy to oblige. Nash was never the same after that. I hope he's well."

Penny took a seat next to Gideon. "He was, until Clara was taken. Why didn't you tell us you were back?"

Hayden sagged in his chair. "I didn't think I'd be well received after what happened. And I had fences to mend with Clara. I can't believe this is happening."

Gideon watched dispassionately as the man wept. He was either genuinely upset, or he was one hell of an actor. "You admit what you did?"

The man wiped his eyes with the handkerchief he had in his pocket. "I messed up. And I panicked. I didn't want to go to jail. And I couldn't admit, at least not back then, that I had failed. So I took what little money there was left and ran. I can't tell you how sorry I was as soon as I did it. But I knew Eldridge would take care of my Clara."

"Was?" Gideon wasn't moved.

"Am. You need to find her. I need to see my baby before I die."

Penny's shock was real. "Die? Are you sick?"

Hayden wiped his eyes. "So the doctors tell me. I have always had a weak heart. It finally caught up to me. I'm supposed to have surgery, but I've been too afraid. I had to make amends first. Clara and I were rebuilding our relationship. She can't be taken from me."

Gideon took Penny's hand and rose. "We'll let you be. Detective McQueen will do everything he can to find her. In the meantime, don't leave town."

Hayden's gaze hardened. "And who are you to say?"

"I'm Gideon Eginhard. Detective Eginhard. And I'm the one who saved Nash."

Hayden's expression didn't change. "I heard about you, of course. Eldridge sent you with Nash to school. Ever the protector. We never had the pleasure of meeting."

"Protector is right. Of the Camhion family. I don't know who is responsible for taking Clara and threatening Penny. But if you have anything to do with it, be assured I'll find out."

"You won't. I assure you."

Gideon led Penny from the room. "No charm today."

Penny glanced back at the closed door. "You don't like him. I can tell. Do you think he had something to do with it?"

"His grief seems real. I'd like to tell you that a father would never do that to his daughter, but I can't. For the family's sake, I hope he isn't involved."

Penny pulled him to a stop. "That's what I like about you. You don't lie, not even to shield us from the painful truth."

Gideon's mouth tightened. "I'm not a shield, Penny. I'm a sword. A weapon. I don't know how to be any other way."

Penny stepped on her toes and kissed him lightly on the mouth. Thankfully, she pulled away before he was tempted to respond. "I don't want you to be anything but what you are."

Gideon didn't know what to say to that, or if he should. Instead, he took her hand and led her back to his desk. He wanted to know more about Hayden Brooks firsthand.

* * *

Penny was bored. She wasn't afraid to admit it. Gideon had spent three hours at the precinct on his computer. Then they'd come back to the apartment where he had spent the last four hours doing much of the same. The notepad next to him was full of notes to prove it. The last thing she wanted to do was distract him. She just didn't know how he did it, staying so focused on the task. She couldn't, and she knew it. She could put presentations together for investors; she could schmooze with the best of them. But she'd go crazy spending hours searching records, investigating the lives of potential suspects, and spending most of her time waiting.

"We should take a break." Gideon rose and stretched.

"You should take a break for the rest of the night. You have to be exhausted. You've spent all day working. And you're supposed to be on vacation."

Gideon dropped down on the sofa and closed his eyes. "I don't know how to do that. I know how to work."

Penny brazenly rose to her knees, slipped one of them between his thighs, and put her hands on his shoulder and chest. "I can help with that."

Gideon was jolted by her touch and jerked to his feet. "Penny."

Penny fell onto the couch. "I don't understand you. I thought you liked me. I thought you were attracted to me. But then you push me away. If I'm wrong, I can handle that. But you have to talk to me."

Gideon's eyes narrowed. "Like you? Is that what you think, Penelope? That I like you?"

Penny's heart dropped to her stomach, and tears stung her eyes. "After the past few days, I did. I guess not."

Penny hadn't gotten more than two steps away from the couch when Gideon spun her into his arms. Penny wanted to pull away from the fury there but was somehow fascinated by his loss of control.

"No, Penelope, I don't like you."

At the finality of those words, Penny burst into tears.

Chapter Ten

Gideon pulled her against his hard body. He held her tight, forcing her to look up at him. "I don't know that there is a word for what I feel, Penny. But 'like' is not it. It's a pale word; a word used by kids who don't know their own minds. So no, I don't like you, Penny. I desire you; I want to devour you. The cold, hard truth is I'm in love with you. And I don't know what to do about it."

Penny's mouth opened, but no words came out. Gideon let her go.

Penny found her voice and grabbed his shoulder. "Don't you walk away from me."

Gideon couldn't help but turn around at her demand. Her cheeks were flushed, and her chest was heaving. "Forget I said anything."

Penny lifted a hand to his cheek. "I don't ever want to forget the first time you told me you love me."

Gideon held still and waited. Penny's eyes were dry this time, and her gaze softened.

Penny lifted her other hand to his cheek. "Gideon, I love you. I have for longer than I realized. If nothing else, this past week has proved it. Who else but someone in love would put up with you?"

Since Gideon couldn't argue her point, he lifted his

hands so that they clasped her wrists. "You're the most beautiful woman I know. And I don't mean your looks. Though they are, too. I won't ever be a sweet, sensitive man. I can't be the hero of your dreams."

Penny vehemently shook her head. "Then I'll be the woman of your dreams. You already dreamed me for you."

Gideon thought back to the drawing, and Penny's soft fingertip tracing the lines of the woman's hair. Gideon wound a lock of her hair around his finger in response to the memory. "I've dreamed of you for years. Be sure, Penny. We can't go back to how things were if we take this any further."

Gideon released her wrists and Penny wound her arms around his neck, lifting herself up so her lips could reach his. "Promise?"

Gideon's arms came around her waist, lifting her off her feet. He nipped at her ear. "Promise."

Gideon heard the word, heard his promise, and swore he'd do anything to make this woman happy. With her feet dangling off the floor, her hips anchored to his, he walked them to his bedroom. He laid her on the bed and looked her over from head to foot. She was wearing a white t-shirt over a pair of faded jeans. And there were her pink glitter sneakers. He slipped one off, then the other. She might as well be wearing silk and lace; she was so beautiful to him.

"Gideon?" Penny rose up on her elbows. "What are you waiting for?"

Gideon didn't need any further urging. He grabbed the hem of his sweater and pulled it over his head. He tossed it aside. He watched with hooded eyes as Penny did the same.

Her bra was lace, much like his fantasy. When she would have removed the bra, he stopped her.

Penny sat still as he slipped one strap down her shoulder and kissed the skin where it had been. He lightly kissed her neck and scraped his teeth over the delicate skin. When Penny shuddered, he did the same on the other side.

"Gideon." Her voice was a whisper.

Gideon's body went rock hard, but he was determined to take this slow. When a fantasy came true, you savored it. His hands went to the hooks of her bra and released it. The pink tips were exactly how he pictured them. He bent his head and kissed the peak while easing her up the mattress so that her head rested on his pillow.

Penny's hands fisted in the length of his hair. She arched her back, begging for the same attention to her other breast.

Gideon obliged. He settled one hand on her damp breast and kissed the other. The smell of her skin was more potent than anything. The scent from her shower this morning had faded, and all he could smell was the sweet scent of her skin. He kissed the underside of one breast, then the other, before kissing his way down her stomach.

Penny released his hair as he made his way to the button of her jeans. "Gideon, I need you. Hurry up."

In response, Gideon ran his fingertip across the skin above her waistband. "Anyone ever tell you how bossy you are? Don't rush me. I've dreamed of this."

"Nash does."

Gideon winced. "Let's not talk about Nash right now."

Penny dropped silent as he unsnapped her jeans. He found matching lace underwear. He stripped off the jeans and her socks in one sweep. Within moments, his mouth was on her belly as his fingers stroked her thighs open. He slipped his tongue under the edge of her underwear, savoring the first real taste of her.

Penny's thighs clenched around his head. "Gideon, I haven't done this before."

Gideon's head popped up. "Sex?"

Penny shook her head. "Not that kind. What you're doing."

Gideon felt his lips curve. "Good. May I?"

When Penny nodded, her expression turned to one of shock as he pulled off her underwear, tossed it aside, and began to kiss her in ways no man had ever kissed her. Gideon savored every second, every taste of her. Her sighs and moans were his undoing. When she convulsed against his mouth, he lost whatever control he had left.

Gideon left her only long enough to get a condom out of the bathroom. She lay there naked and dazed. Her eyes were hooded as she watched him return to her. He rolled the condom on and returned to the warmth between her legs, this time with the part of him that ached the most.

But Gideon, before he took the irrevocable step, needed to hear the words. "Say you love me. Again, Penelope."

Penny didn't have to be asked twice. Her thighs tightened around him in anticipation and pulled his head down to her. Her breath tickled his ear. "I love you, Gideon. More than anything. And if you don't finish what you started, I'll kill you."

Gideon kissed her hard and slid into her with one quick stroke. "Yes, ma'am."

Penny's body tightened. "Not now."

Gideon held still. "What 'not now' do you mean? It's a bit late."

Penny kissed him hard enough to leave a mark on his lip. "Don't make jokes. This is not a laughing matter."

"No, it sure isn't."

Gideon's hands flattened on the mattress beside her hips, and he withdrew, but only for a moment. He never wanted this moment to end. But Penny had different ideas. Her nails dug into his back, and her hips arched to take him deeper. With another deep kiss, he quickened his pace, relishing every squeeze of her body, every tug, and every surge. Burying his face in her soft hair, he lost all control. He felt as much as heard the climax that took over her body. Wanting it to last but unable to control it, he erupted inside her, this first time beyond anything he had dreamed.

It was dark in the room when he had enough energy to rouse his body enough to roll off of her. He was so much bigger than she was, though she had not felt delicate as she accepted and returned his thrusts. She was perfect in every way, and it scared him.

Penny kissed his chest. "I can hear the gears turning."

Gideon wrapped his arms around her, bringing her against his chest. He wanted to feel her damp skin against him. Unable to help himself, he kissed her brow and stroked her back in long sweeps. She was the most amazing thing that had ever happened to him. He wasn't sure what he had done to deserve Penny's love, but he didn't want to question it. He wanted to savor the feel of her skin against his, her soft hair on his chest. He loved her more than he had words to express, and this was a moment he thought he would only ever dream of.

Penny kissed his chin. "A penny for your thoughts?"

Gideon felt her smiling as she kissed his chin again. He knew he should say something, but words eluded him. So he said the only thing he could come up with. "I love you."

Penny sighed and relaxed against him. "Our mothers will be happy, I think."

Gideon thought of his mother. She would approve. She had always been his champion, even when he was in the wrong. She'd tell him everyone made mistakes. And that smart people learned from them. And then she'd tell him she'd box his ears if he did it again. He never made the same mistake twice.

He wasn't so sure about Victoria. While he did think of her as a second mother, and Nash as his brother, he never once thought of Penny as a sister. The day he first saw her, he wanted her. It was as if his soul was drawn to the beauty of hers. But would Victoria approve? He wasn't so sure.

When Penny nudged him, he realized he hadn't answered. "My mother will. I'm not sure about yours."

Penny folded her arms under her chin so she could see his eyes. "Trust me. She loves me and wants me to be happy. She knows exactly how I feel about you. Though I did deny it at first. But she saw me crying the first time you kissed me. It was hard not to confide."

Gideon frowned at her. "You cried?"

Penny reassured him. "The good kind."

Gideon spoke without thinking. "Nash gave me his blessing."

Penny poked him in the chest. "What?"

Gideon saw the outrage on her face. He couldn't help himself. He laughed. He laughed so hard his stomach hurt. "It's a guy thing. I didn't dare make the moves on my best friend's sister without it."

Penny pouted. "I made the first move, remember?"

Gideon pulled her closer so he could give her a soft kiss. "I remember. I'll remember until the day I die."

Penny's lips softened on his; she murmured against his lips. "You can be romantic when you try."

Gideon didn't have a response to that, either. But he was glad he'd made her happy. "You should sleep. We both should."

Penny laid her head on his chest and closed her eyes. "Can I stay here?"

Gideon looked down at the woman draped across his chest. She had already dozed off when he spoke. "Until the day I die."

* * *

Gideon woke early in the morning to a loud knock on his front door. Gideon eased a still-sleeping Penny off his chest and grabbed the gun he'd tucked in the nightstand. He heard three male voices behind the door. Gideon shouted through the door. "One sec."

Gideon returned to the bedroom to put his gun back and found Penny rubbing the sleep out of her eyes. "We have company."

Penny's eyes slid over a naked Gideon. "Tell them to go

away."

Gideon kept his eyes off Penny's curves under the sheets. "I can't. One of them is your brother."

Penny let out a very unladylike expletive. "Of all the days."

Gideon had the same thought. He went to his dresser and pulled out some fresh clothes. He supposed there wasn't much he could do about the fact that it looked like he had just left the bed he and Penny had shared. The best he could do was close the door behind him and pretend he hadn't just rolled a naked Penny off his chest.

Gideon let the three men in. "I wasn't expecting you to come here."

Nash dropped down on the couch, Isaac went to make coffee, and Trenton stood by Isaac, telling him what to do. But it was Nash who held Gideon's attention. He could tell his friend hadn't been sleeping. Anger at the situation settled in his gut. "Man, you need to rest."

Nash rubbed his face, one that was sporting the beginnings of a beard. "I wanted to see Penny. I video chatted with my parents earlier. Grandma is driving them nuts. She wants to drive here and find out who took Clara and take him out herself. Never mind that she's ninety years old."

Gideon took the cup of coffee Isaac handed him and handed it to Nash. "I knew there was a reason I adore that woman. She brings new meaning to the word feisty."

Nash accepted the cup, though his stomach was already churning from the four cups he drank earlier. "It's where Penny gets it from. Where is she?"

Gideon glanced at the bedroom door. "Probably getting dressed by now. You guys make enough racket wherever you go; she must be awake in there."

Trenton dropped next to Nash. "That's my line."

Isaac took the third spot. "Trenton never learned to share as a child."

Trenton's blond brow rose at that, but didn't comment.

Nash set the unwanted coffee on the table. "Is Penny okay? Sleeping?"

Gideon tore his gaze from the bedroom door. "Better than you are. I wasn't kidding; you need sleep."

Nash slammed a frustrated fist on the couch arm. "I'll sleep when we find Clara. She might be a pain in the ass, but she's family. And your detective friend isn't any closer to finding her. Are you?"

Gideon wished he had a better answer, but he didn't. "We're putting the pieces together."

Penny slowly opened the bedroom door. "Is it safe to come out?"

Nash rose and embraced his sister. He looked at her face, then looked at Gideon, then back at his sister. "Damn, it's about time."

Trenton practically spit out his coffee. He looked at Penny and saw what they all saw. A woman with swollen lips, tousled hair, and a t-shirt on inside out. His lips twitched. "You might want to fix your shirt."

Penny looked down and turned crimson red. She pulled out of Nash's arms and slammed the door behind her.

Isaac, the sensible one, broke the ice. "Hey, congrats. I'll second Nash. It's about time."

Nash pointed a finger at Isaac. "Don't congratulate him, you ass. That's my sister he's sleeping with."

Trenton shook his head. "I figured the two of you already had something going on the side. Penny always dances around the subject when you come up in conversation."

Gideon looked at his friend. He cleared his throat. "I thought something was going on with you two."

Trenton looked stunned. "Me? Me and Penny? Now that is funny. I'd drive her nuts if she had to live with me."

Nash realized what the two men were talking about. Nash pointed at Gideon. "You thought Penny and Trenton were a couple? I thought you were smarter than that."

Trenton feigned insult. "Why not me? I'm a catch."

"For fish maybe. Or would that be a worm?" That was Isaac.

Trenton snickered. "Wait until Penny hears this."

"She already did." Penny pointed at Gideon. "Can I talk to you?"

The three men pretended like they weren't listening, but it was hard not to in the small apartment. Penny took Gideon's wrist, dragged him into the bedroom, and slammed the door.

Penny poked Gideon in the chest. "You thought I was sleeping with Trenton?"

Gideon realized she was mad. "Yes and no."

Penny poked him again. "What kind of answer is that?"

Gideon responded honestly. "The only one I have."

Penny sputtered, but then her eyes narrowed. "So you took me to bed, even though you thought I might be sleeping with one of your best friends?"

Gideon tucked a strand of hair behind her ear. "You said you loved me. It was all I needed to hear. Though I am glad I don't have to kill Trenton."

Penny's gaze softened, then hardened. "You're not going to charm your way out of this."

Gideon pulled her into his arms. "You said I didn't have any charm."

Penny, forgetting the men were in the next room, rubbed herself against him. "You have your moments."

Gideon was about to kiss her when loud coughs came from the living room. He sighed and let her go. "We should go out there."

"Ugh. Do we have to?" Penny reluctantly let Gideon go. "It just occurred to me that I'll be seeing a lot more of the four of you."

Gideon stopped. "Will you?"

Penny touched his arm. "Bet on it."

Gideon opened the door. "You three need to learn subtlety. It is not your strong suit."

Nash's head lay against the couch cushion. "You can date her. You can marry her. You can sleep with her. But I do not, ever, want the details. Clear?"

Penny crossed her arms over her chest. "I don't need your permission."

Nash smiled at his baby sister. "You have it anyway. I need to sleep."

Penny glanced at Gideon, who nodded. She slipped out of the room.

"You can sleep here. Penny will make up the bed."

Nash's eyes were closing. "Oh, man. That is so wrong."

Gideon agreed, but it was the only bed. "It's either that or the floor."

Nash's voice was fading. "Tried that. The floor is too hard. I think I'm getting old. We used to be able to sleep anywhere."

Trenton patted his friend's knee. "So we did."

Five minutes later, Penny waved at Gideon, and Isaac and Trenton helped Nash to his feet. Gideon and Penny watched as they helped Nash out of his shoes and put him under the covers.

Isaac closed the door behind Trenton. "I remember one other time we had to put Nash to bed. What a bender that was."

Trenton remembered. "And over a woman, no less. No offense, Penny."

Penny gave Trenton a side hug. "None taken. You can think of me as just one of the guys."

Trenton slapped Gideon on the back. "You know you now owe me a date on Fridays. Something tells me you're not going to let Penny come over for movie night."

Gideon saw Penny watching him and waiting for his response. "Penny can do what she wants."

Penny seemed satisfied with the answer until Gideon spoke again.

"But I'll be there, too."

Trenton slapped Gideon on the back. "That's my boy!"

* * *

Penny never spent a lot of time with the quartet as a whole. Usually it was just Nash and one or two of them. It was nice to watch these four men interact with each other. They were all different, and yet they meshed. There was a harmony to the way they interacted. She knew Nash thought of them all as brothers. And though she didn't know for a fact, she was sure these men were also his confidants. She had wanted to cry when she saw all three of them taking care of Nash.

When she had emerged from the bedroom, her eyes had gone straight to Gideon, not Nash. That in and of itself was a momentous moment for her, though she doubted Gideon noticed. Nash was not the priority, but Gideon. Gideon, who if she had her way, would one day be her husband and the father of her children. And wasn't that the kicker. She was in love with Gideon Eginhard, and he was in love with her. It was hard to imagine a time when she wasn't. She wasn't glad she had been attacked, but she was glad that it was Gideon who had come to her rescue. Getting to this stage in their relationship might have taken much longer had they not been forced together.

But teasing and playtime were over, and Nash, who might have only slept a couple of hours, at least had gotten some rest. The dark circles under his eyes were still there, but he wasn't slurring any words or wobbling on his feet. Now he was pacing.

"Hayden Brooks. I can't believe he surfaced. Does Dad know?"

Penny interrupted. "I wasn't going to tell him unless we have to. But if Gideon doesn't find any dirt on him, we might need to. He's dying, or so he says."

Nash continued pacing. "He did have a bad heart. I remember the little pills he kept in his pocket. Maybe karma is finally catching up to him."

Penny continued. "He said he's been in touch with Clara these past couple of years. Said he was making amends, or something to that effect."

Nash scoffed at that. "Amends. If he wants to make amends, he can return all the money he stole. And he can make a public apology for trying to smear the Camhion name with his pathetic scheme."

Gideon turned to face the group. His back had been to them as he contemplated what he had learned about Hayden. "I can't believe I didn't know about this. But so far, he's clean. And Detective McQueen says he has an alibi. He was in the middle of an echocardiogram when Clara was taken."

Nash stopped pacing. "What else?"

Gideon summarized what he had read. "Two men, both dressed in suits, entered the Camhion mansion at approximately 8:25 pm. Both men mingled with the guests, likely casing the place. They stopped, had a plate of food, downed two glasses of champagne each, and then met back up at the south entrance. From there, one man pulled a bottle out and pulled off a stopper. The other man stuffed a rag in it, lit it, and tossed it. Most of the guests had their backs to the door, so it's not likely anyone realized someone had thrown a cocktail. The table lit, the curtains lit, and the fire started to spread. In the ensuing chaos, both men entered the hall, pointed to Clara, whose back was to them, and the larger of the two grabbed her. The second wrapped a towel over her head. It is unlikely she saw her kidnappers at that time. As people were trying to get out of the house, the two men slipped back out the south entrance and hopped into a white van. The caterer's logo was on the van, likely stolen from one of the other vans to make it look like the caterer was leaving."

Penny and Nash both spoke at the same time. "Was she hurt?"

Gideon didn't let any of his emotions show. "She fought them. Tried to claw the towel from her face. One of the men hit her on the head with the butt of a gun. She slumped and was carried to the van."

Penny turned to Gideon and wrapped her arms around him.

It didn't get past Nash's notice that Penny had gone to Gideon and not him. "We have to find Clara."

Isaac clasped Nash's shoulder. "Gideon will find her. Who do we know that would do this? If it's not Hayden, who else?"

Gideon continued. "I hate to say it, but Hayden could have paid someone. We know one man tried to grab Penny. But it's possible there was a second man waiting. We never saw him, but given what the police saw on the security cameras, an accomplice in Penny's attempted abduction is likely. Penny, I'll need you to look at the two men and see if one of them could be the man who tried to grab you."

Penny let Gideon go and turned so he could pull up the pictures of the men. The first one didn't resemble her attacker at all. The second one did. His face was swollen and bruised from where her elbow hit his face, but the eyebrows and eyes were unmistakable. "The second one. The one with the bushy eyebrows. Put a hat on him, and that's the guy."

Gideon tapped a few keys. "I've let Detective McQueen know. We don't know who the men are yet, but he's already running their faces. They were not wearing gloves at the scene. It would have stood out too much. And they obviously didn't know they were on camera. They didn't try to hide their faces. I had Eldridge put cameras in while everyone was out so no one else would know about them in case something like this happened."

Nash continued his pacing, his tired brain just then picking up what he had said about cameras. "You had cameras installed? Inside the house? I guess I'd complain it's an invasion of privacy, but we got the bastards on camera."

Gideon closed the pictures. "No one was looking at the footage, at least not until the party. And there weren't any cameras in the sensitive areas, like the bedrooms or bathrooms."

Penny didn't like it but didn't say so. "I suppose I should be glad, too. Will there be evidence after the fire?"

Gideon hoped there would be. "I'm hoping there will at least be prints on the back door. And the bottle didn't break into small pieces. We might be able to get a fingerprint off one of the larger pieces that were collected. And if we're really lucky, we'll have their mugshots and fingerprints in the records. Guys like this are generally not that smart; they commit a crime, do time, and get out to do it again."

"Sounds like a pair of peaches." Trenton turned to Penny. "We should probably get out of your hair."

Gideon seconded that. "I need to check some things. And Nash, you need some real sleep. Trenton, go buy air mattresses."

Trenton saluted. "Will do, boss."

Penny hugged everyone as they left, giving Nash an extra-long one. "Please get some rest. Don't make me worry about you."

Nash kissed his sister's cheek and mimicked Trenton. "Will do, Boss."

Penny pushed him out the door and closed it behind him. "I love him, I really do. But he can be such a smart aleck."

Gideon set the locks. "It's one of his charms."

Penny leaned against him. "He has a lot of them. And most are fake. But despite that, I can see why the four of you get along so well. You complement each other."

Gideon lifted Penny into his arms. "You think so?"

Penny wound her arms around his neck. "Yep. And you know what else I think?"

Gideon laid her on the bed and followed her down. "No."

Penny shivered when his hands slid under her shirt. "I really like it when you pick me up like that. Very romantic. Even charming."

Gideon pulled her shirt over her head. "I aim to please."

And please her, he did.

Chapter Eleven

Gideon left Penny sleeping. He sincerely hoped Nash was asleep back at Cantwell's office. Both brother and sister were looking a little ragged. Though he supposed, as far as Penny went, that was partly his fault. He kept trying to drum up regret. Or at least a little self-loathing that he couldn't keep his hands to himself. But his heart wasn't in it. Penny made him feel amazing. And while the sex was great, too, her faith in him, her belief that he could be charming and romantic, made him feel like the hero she deserved.

Gideon pulled out the file folder on Penny's attack from the drawer. He added additional notes to the file that the men who had taken Clara were not young men. Often, people who did that kind of work were young punks looking for a quick buck, ignoring the fact that kidnapping would land them in jail for years. But the cameras had picked up their faces, mature faces. Gideon pulled the copy of the sketch of Penny's attacker and put it next to the picture of the man from the video footage. The eyes were a perfect match, as were the eyebrows.

"It's him."

Gideon almost jumped. He hadn't heard her come up behind him. A first for him. "You're supposed to be asleep."

Penny slipped onto his lap. "You weren't there."

Gideon's body leaped to attention at the feel of Penny's bottom rubbing on his lap, but he stayed in the chair. "I think you're right. About the man, I mean. You described him very well to the artist. It might not impress a jury, but it should be enough to convince a judge for a warrant after we figure out his name."

Penny picked up the photo to get a better look. "Do you think these guys were hired? That Hayden hired them?"

Gideon held her hips still. "It's possible. It's been years since they'd spoken, so why did he show up in Clara's life the past couple of years and try to rebuild a relationship with her? Assuming that's true. But if he is involved, why now? If he's been back two years, why not threaten you and attempt to kidnap you two years ago? For a man like Hayden Brooks, money would be a big motivator, and Clara has done well these past years working for Camhion."

"Maybe he wanted Clara's trust first. He could have learned a lot about us through her. She is family. And she might not be as cautious with her father as she might be with someone on the outside. Maybe he used Clara to learn about us and chose now to strike. But why kidnap Clara?"

Gideon hated that the words he was going to say could be the truth. "He might want to eliminate his source of information. Clara could testify against him that she was the one who fed him the information. She wouldn't suspect her father when the letters came. And if he's as sick as he says, he wouldn't be able to grab her himself. And because she's his daughter, he might not be able to do the deed himself either."

Penny shuddered and tried not to cry. "You think Clara is dead, don't you?"

Gideon rubbed her back. "It's a possibility, but there are others. She could be very much alive. She could be being held someplace until Hayden is ready to make his next move. The police found him, and maybe he hadn't thought they would. He could be lying low, playing the grieving father, in order to push suspicion away from him. McQueen already confirmed his alibi. He went to the ER around six. He was getting tests at the time of the abduction. He's on multiple hospital security cameras, so there really is no way he was there when Clara was abducted. But it seems convenient that he was in the ER when she was taken."

"What does Detective McQueen think?"

Gideon's answer was brief. "He thinks I'm paranoid."

Penny furrowed her brows. "Why?"

Gideon knew it was time to come clean, to show her everything. "This."

Penny watched him open the drawer and pull out a second file. He handed it to her.

The first thing Penny saw was the article on her grandfather's murder. She stared at it numbly. "You're investigating this?"

Gideon eased Penny off his lap. "Yeah. I have been since before I joined the academy. I used it as my case file study. The Cold Case Unit is letting me help."

Penny pulled a sketch out of the folder. Then another. And another. "I never saw this. Is this the guy who killed my grandfather?"

Gideon gently took the sketches from her. "I don't know. But he is the man who had Nash."

Penny came closer, her fingers going to the scars on his face. She hardly noticed them anymore. "He did this to you."

Gideon jerked away from her touch. "I know they're not pretty. But I don't need sympathy."

Penny folded her arms across her chest. "You won't get any from me. I told your mother, and I'll tell you. I'm glad you have them. My brother is alive because of what you did, and those scars seem like a small price to pay for his life. So I don't pity you."

When Gideon stood, he could see his reflection in the mirror in the bathroom. "Is that what you see?"

Penny crossed to him again. "I see life when I see them. I don't suppose that's how you see them."

Gideon turned his eyes away from his reflection. "I never forget they are there. People stare. It's fine. I get it. I can't hide them. But the scars remind me of something important."

"I can't imagine what. Other than what must have been a very scary night."

Gideon dropped his gaze to the picture he was holding. The truth of that night tumbled out. "I was in an alley after I'd snuck out after bedtime. I was going to rob the liquor store. I had a gun in my pocket. It wasn't loaded, but I thought it would scare the clerk enough to turn over the cash. I had a ski mask in my other pocket so no one would see my face. My knees were knocking so badly that I was afraid I'd fumble it. But I'd seen enough television to know how it was done. I was only a block from the liquor store when I heard muffled yells coming from across the alley."

"Gideon." Penny's voice was a whisper in reaction to the pain she could hear in his voice.

Gideon ignored her, lost in the memory. "I thought the boy was probably my age. I saw the man had a knife right before he tucked it in his pocket. I knew the gun in my pocket was useless, but he didn't. I was within a few feet of him when he saw me. Instead of pulling out the gun, I jumped him. I didn't hesitate. I didn't think. I was big for my age but wasn't as strong as I thought. I knocked the knife out of his hand, and I grabbed a broken liquor bottle. I saw that on television, too, how to use a bottle as a weapon. But the man had the advantage of age and strength, and he got the bottle away from me. In the tussle, the bottle raked across my forehead. The adrenaline was still pumping. I didn't give up. The second cut slashed me above my eyebrow and down my cheek. Nash couldn't scream with his mouth duct-taped, but I could. Instead of going for the kidnapper again, I dove for the knife. I was screaming the entire time. Lights came on in the apartments. When I rolled onto my back with the knife, the man looked down at me. He smiled and started coming toward me. I finally remembered the gun. I tossed the knife and pulled the gun out of my pocket and aimed it at him. He wasn't smiling anymore. Shouts were coming from the apartment windows, and the man decided it was time to run. He saluted me, like a police or military officer. And grabbed the knife and ran into the dark."

Penny stayed where she was, listening to the full story,

one she had only heard sanitized.

"The doctor who cleaned and stitched me up was worried about an infection, but said I'd been very lucky not to have lost an eye. By then the drugs were kicking in, and I wasn't feeling much of anything. I remember Victoria coming in. Her soft blonde hair was in a twist, and she was wearing a sparkling white dress. I thought she was an angel. Tears were sparkling on her lashes. When Victoria came in, saw me lying in the bed, my face stitched up with dried blood all over me, she clutched me to her. My mom wasn't there yet, and I clung to her. I think I loved her from that moment. She promised me that she and her husband would do anything to help. Nash was in the room next to mine. I could hear his father trying to get his son to tell him what had happened. I never heard Nash say a word. I knew without asking that the woman standing before me was his mother."

Penny tried to touch him, but he jerked back. "My mom adores you."

"Penny, I wanted money. Once the drugs started to wear off, I saw her, and I saw money. I thought this was the big score I needed. The score my family needed. I could practically taste it."

Penny held her hand out to him, then dropped it to her side when he ignored it. "But you didn't take it. I know you didn't. You went to school with Nash as payment, a small one compared to what we owed you. A debt we could not repay."

Gideon rubbed the scars with his fingers. "No. I didn't. I found out about your grandfather, and it made me sick.

Sick that I was the type of person to take money from a family when their grandfather had been murdered. Sick that I was the type of person who would rob a liquor store and terrorize a young clerk who was barely making minimum wage."

Penny couldn't stand it, and she threw herself at him, willing him to listen. "You are not that man. The boy might have tried, but you didn't succeed. You did the right thing. Whether by design or decision, you didn't go back and rob that liquor store. You didn't take the money my parents would have given you. And I guarantee it would have been more than a thirteen-year-old brain could imagine. You saved a life. Maybe it saved yours, too."

Gideon felt tears choke him. "It wasn't enough. I wasn't enough. He got away. A murderer got away. I need to find the man who did this to Nash, to Cormac. To you and your parents."

Penny shed the tears he couldn't. "And you."

Gideon clutched her to him. "I'm not the man you need, but Penny, I need you so much it scares me."

Penny gently placed her hands on his face and lifted his eyes to her. "I'm not afraid of you. I admit, you gave me a start when we met the first time. I'd heard about the scars, but I had never seen them. And you, you were glaring at me, which didn't help. But I never felt fear. You're just not that type of man."

Gideon held her against him.

* * *

Penny saw the argument about to come. So she hushed him the only way she knew how. She used the grip on his face to bring his mouth to hers. He didn't object; didn't pull back. She breathed her love for him against his mouth, loving those lips, teasing him with soft kisses.

Penny took a step, forcing him to take one backward. With her arms guiding him, she walked him to the bedroom. She pushed him into a seated position on the end of the bed. "I'm going to make love to you, Gideon, until you can't remember anything you just told me. I don't care why you were in that alley. I don't care what you think you are. I know who you are. You're the man I'm in love with, and I couldn't love you any less, even if you had robbed that store. Or had taken the money my parents would have given you. Or never set foot in the private school with Nash."

Gideon's eyes never left hers as she stripped off his shirt. Her trembling fingers then went to the buttons of his jeans. He wore nothing underneath them, and she used the opportunity to explore him the way he had her. "Lift up so I can get these off."

Gideon obeyed.

Penny stripped off the jeans. She then stripped off the nightgown she'd been wearing when she came out to find him. She wore nothing underneath. "Now lie down."

Again, Gideon obeyed.

Penny ran her palms over his skin from the tops of his feet all the way to his shoulders. His legs were long and roped with muscle. His abdomen was flat, and his large chest was spattered with soft black hair. His skin was a deep bronze, so much darker than hers. Her hands looked pale and tiny as they smoothed over his body. It was with a sense of awe that she discovered she had so much power over him. His body shuddered underneath her palms, his eyes narrowed on her, helpless as he watched her.

She found his nipples with her teeth, biting and soothing them in turn. She then straddled him, teasing him with the heat of her body. Not wanting to be apart from him for another second, she braced herself on his chest and eased herself onto him. When he was fully seated inside her, she let out a sigh of satisfaction and her head tipped back. She stayed still, focusing on him, the tiny shivers that wracked her body, and the small pulsations she could feel with him inside her.

This time it was Gideon's turn to beg, but Penny wasn't having it. She looked down at him. He was so much bigger than she was. His body was hard and lean, and the strength in him should frighten her. But she didn't fear him; she knew deep down he would never hurt her. From the scars on his face to the love she could see in his eyes to the powerful body that was now hers, everything about him aroused her. "This time it's my fantasy. And I'm going to enjoy it."

Penny brought his hands to her breasts and held them there. She rode him slowly, taking her time. She could feel when he was going to go over the edge, and she would ease back. She was tormenting both of them, but she didn't care.

Gideon's voice was gravelly when he spoke, his breath coming in deep inhalations. "You're killing me."

Penny slid further down, sealing their bodies once again. "Good. You want to be punished? I'm just the woman to do it."

Penny played and teased him a while longer until she couldn't take it anymore. "Now, you can have me."

The guttural growl that came from Gideon's throat was one she would never forget. He slipped out of her, flipped her on her back, and plunged back in. It was only seconds before both of them were clinging to each other, both of their releases singing through them in unison.

Their harsh breaths were the only sounds in the room. After a few moments, Penny pushed his shoulders until he rolled over onto his back. She sat up for a moment and gazed down at him. His dark eyelashes were lying against his cheeks. With love overwhelming her, she lay down so that her head was on his chest. She stayed that way until his breathing was even, and then she, too, drifted off to sleep.

* * *

Good things never seemed to last; at least that was Gideon's first thought when the phone rang. Penny's damp breath was stirring the hairs on his chest. He had been awake for a while, just listening to her breathe. He was not ready to get up yet and face a new day. He wanted to just lie here and remember last night. He wanted to remember how she made him feel as if he were forgiven somehow. And he would never forget Penny's face when she said she was the woman to exact punishment. And what a punishment it was.

She was right, though. He knew deep down she was. He thought Penny would run from the truth of that night. He should have known better. But he knew it was time to tell Penny the entire truth; one he had never shared before. His mother had an idea that whatever he had been up to was not good. But armed robbery, even if the gun wasn't loaded, was not what she would think.

He had withheld the truth for two reasons. One, he wasn't stupid and didn't want to end up in jail for having an illegal firearm. He had found it in the park and at the time he had slipped it into his book bag for safekeeping. And as the man of the family, it could come in handy. But the second, and most important reason, was that he didn't want to hurt his mother any more than he already had. The detective who had questioned him had not told his mother about the gun. Other than the police, Nash and the kidnapper were the only ones who knew about it. The detective had taken it from him, handed it off to one of the officers for safekeeping, and continued his questioning. The relief he had felt, and the respect for that officer, never dimmed.

Penny stirred. "Is that mine or yours?"

Gideon shifted under her, enjoying the shift of her skin over his. "Yours. I'd tell you to ignore it, but it's probably Nash or your parents."

"I talked to my parents yesterday while you were in the shower. It's probably Nash."

But it wasn't Nash on the phone.

Penny sat up and awkwardly slid off him and to her feet. "Clara. Where are you?"

Gideon immediately sat up and called McQueen. The man answered. Gideon didn't bother with pleasantries.

"Clara on Penny's phone."

"On it."

"Clara, please, where are you? Are you hurt? Are you alone?"

Gideon gently took the phone from Penny and put it on speaker.

Clara's voice was low and hard to hear on the static-filled line. "It's dark. Not alone. Want money."

Penny clutched Gideon's arm that held the phone. "Who wants money? Clara, please."

"Two men. Can't see them. They want money. They said they'd kill me. Please, Penny, please. Help me."

Gideon set the phone down and began tugging on the clothes Penny had tossed on the floor. "Keep her talking," he mouthed.

"I'll help you; I promise."

"Bank account to come to you in email. Send the money and they'll give you the address where I am. Hurry, Penny, please."

"I will, Clara. I promise."

Penny burst into tears when the phone line went dead.

Gideon went and grabbed his laptop and brought it to her. "Email."

Penny was trembling but was able to get to her email and log in. There was a new email. "Should I open it?"

Gideon laid his hand over hers while handing her a notepad and pencil. "Write your email and password down for McQueen. He'll have the analysts open it."

The words were legible, but barely. Her hands would not stop trembling, and tears dripped onto the pad.

Gideon helped her to her feet. "Go ahead and get dressed. We'll head over to the precinct."

Penny grabbed his arm, her nails digging into the muscles of his forearms. "We have to pay. We have to get her back. We can't lose her, too. We need to call Nash."

No words would soothe her, so he gently tucked her against him and held her for a moment while she struggled for control. When the trembling had mostly subsided, he pulled her away so he could look into her eyes. "Please, get dressed."

Penny nodded and did as he asked. Gideon had to help her tie her sneakers when her hands refused to cooperate.

The bullpen was a bustle of activity. McQueen saw them first. "Eginhard."

Gideon had left Penny with one of the officers. She had protested while struggling to hold back tears, but then relented. He wanted to know what was in that email before he told Penny. If there was anything other than a ransom demand, he didn't want her to see it.

"What does it say?" Gideon leaned over the desk of the analyst who was trying to trace it.

McQueen responded. "Generic email. It was on a timed send that was scheduled using a computer at the library. No cameras, unfortunately. Some nonsense about invasion of privacy."

Gideon grunted at that. It sounded like a good thing until it didn't help your case. "Basic demand?"

"Bold, I'd say. I don't know how much money the Camhion family has, and no doubt it's a lot. But anyone who demands fifty million dollars is out of their mind.

Even if the family has that kind of money, I'd bet it's tied up in investments."

Gideon would agree, but he knew a bit about investments, and that kind of cash can be had when needed by people like Eldridge Camhion. "Penny doesn't have that. I know Clara doesn't. I can reach out to Nash or Eldridge. Nash used to gamble; I wouldn't be surprised if he still has cash stashed for high-stakes games."

McQueen whistled. "I'll let you make that call."

Somehow that didn't surprise Gideon at all. "Give me a few."

Gideon went to a quiet place to make the call. "Hi, Nash, it's Gideon."

Gideon could hear Nash gritting his teeth. "I know who it is, Eginhard. Has there been a break?"

"Ransom demand. Just saw it. The call came into Penny's phone, but I wanted to make sure it was the real deal before I called you."

Nash's tone picked up in urgency. "She's alive?"

"She is. She's the one who called."

Nash's next question was expected. "How much?"

"Fifty mil."

Nash swore loud and clear. Other voices began talking behind him. "Gideon says fifty mil."

The voices got louder.

Gideon hushed them. "Listen. It's a lot. More than I thought. It's up to you what you want to do. But you know better than anyone that payment doesn't guarantee a return."

The line was silent as the three men absorbed what he

had said.

"I'll pay it." Nash's voice was firm over the line. "We have to try."

Gideon went back to the detective and the analyst so she could set up the transfer of funds to an account that the police could track. Then he went and found Penny.

She stood when he came in. "Well?"

Gideon nodded at the officer she was with and waved her over. He held her as he led her to his desk. "Nash is putting up the ransom money. It will be a few hours yet."

Penny let Gideon ease her into a chair. "I don't know if I should be relieved or more scared."

Gideon rubbed her back. "Neither. Now we have to wait."

It seemed like hours before the money was finally ready to be transferred to the account. The police officers working the case were all waiting for the green light to send the money and reply to the email.

"Have you found her yet?" Hayden Brooks burst into the bullpen.

An officer blocked him, but McQueen waved him through. "Not yet, Mr. Brooks. We told you we would reach out once we knew more."

Hayden made a chopping motion with his hand into his fist. "I'm not going to sit around and wait to see if you find her. Find her!"

McQueen nodded at the officer who had blocked him. "Relax, Mr. Brooks, or Officer Mahoney will remove you."

As if all his energy had given out, Hayden's knees buckled. The officer held him up and led him to some benches off to the side. He left the man there.

Gideon saw Penny watching Hayden. "Don't, Penny."

Penny kept her eyes on Hayden. "I think he really is sick. And I think he's really scared."

Gideon wasn't sold, but he also didn't discount the possibility.   But he'd rather Penny didn't waste her sympathies on him. Gideon had no patience with men who stole, especially from people who already had very little to begin with. Gideon had dug into the failed land deal. And Eldridge had sent him the files from the private detective. Hayden took money from elderly people, people with young children, and people who simply could not afford to lose what little they had invested.

"Detective Eginhard." Captain Barnes approached. "I see you're still involved in this."

"Clara Brooks is Penny's cousin. Nash is fronting the ransom. I'm involved."

Barnes pointed to McQueen. "We're going to send Eginhard in with your team. We have a fire and a shooting to deal with. I need everyone on board who's available." He turned to Gideon.   "We'll talk about your continued investigation into this matter when you're back from vacation. Suit up."

Gideon turned to Penny. "Stay here. No matter what, don't leave. I don't care if Nash shows up; you stay."

"Will you call Nash to come?"

Gideon shook his head. "I don't need to. No doubt Nash, Trenton, and Isaac are already on their way here. Just promise me you'll stay put."

"I promise."

Gideon didn't kiss her or say goodbye. This was what he did for a living, and he prayed she could live with it.

It wasn't long before the email came through with an address. Detective McQueen addressed the team, giving each group their assignment. The location was quickly pulled up and assessed, and a plan was made to infiltrate.

Chapter Twelve

The address was a building across town. No doubt the perps chose the spot for the ambiance. Most of the light bulbs in the streetlamps had been busted out. Trash lined the streets and alleys. And to top it off, the building was an abandoned warehouse. It would take time to search it.

McQueen had opted for obvious instead of covert, with sirens going and spotlights set up. He split the men into four groups, one to enter on each side of the warehouse. Gideon headed up group two. They moved around to the north side of the building, kicking in the side door. It appeared to be a reception area that was now littered with garbage and gang symbols spray-painted all over the walls. He didn't want to know what the smell was that emanated from the building. He wouldn't be surprised if they were not alone. The abandoned structure was perfect for squatters, the homeless, addicts, and anyone who needed a place to get off the streets. And a great place for all sorts of rats and other vermin to live.

But as the team did a sweep, no one was found, though the rats were plentiful. Gideon opened his mic. "North entrance is clear. We're going into the main area."

"Copy. Nothing on the south."

"West clear."

"East clear."

Gideon closed his mic and moved the team further into the darkened building. There was no electricity in the building, so it was dark and deep shadows concealed old furniture and more garbage. Their flashlights swept paths through the gloom. Other than the dirt the team was kicking up by walking through the grime and the rats scurrying from the light, nothing else stirred. No one was hiding in the shadows. The team was checking in, and there was no sign of Clara.

The teams met up in the middle. McQueen wiped the sweat and grime from his brow. "Where else?"

"We need light. There could be stairs, closets, or rooms we can't see."

McQueen agreed. "Team four get spotlights in here."

When there was enough light, the teams started a second sweep. Gideon stopped and stayed still, listening and waiting for any sound, any movement. He thought he heard a noise. It was faint, but it was there. He gestured to his team to remain still. He heard it again.

"Two o'clock." Gideon raised his gun and moved toward the sound. There were tall metal shelves along the wall. He swept his hand, and the team moved in.

The men grabbed and moved the shelves. "There's a door here, sir."

Gideon took point. He and two other men covered the opening while a third yanked the door open. A foul odor that made them cough wafted from the opening. "Move."

There was a narrow corridor, barely able to fit Gideon's shoulders. At the end, a pale, blonde woman lay bound on the floor wearing nothing more than a dirty evening gown. A quick sweep past where she lay showed they were alone. With officers at his back, he dropped to his knees. "She's alive. We need to move her. There is no way a paramedic is getting to her in here."

Gideon took a knife out of his pocket and cut the plastic ties that held her arms and legs behind her. He was rewarded with a moan, which he took to be a good sign. She was out, but not completely. He took his police jacket off after handing the knife to the officer behind him. He did a quick assessment. Nothing appeared to be broken, though there was a lot of blood. Clara's face was painfully swollen, her wrists and ankles bruised. Shifting behind her so he could get a grip, Gideon lifted Clara into his arms.

Her eyes opened. "Gideon. I knew you'd come."

The officer leading the group opened his mic and requested a paramedic be called into the warehouse. He also kept the flashlight high enough so Gideon could see to maneuver her out of the cramped space. He ignored the whimpers coming from Clara, concentrating on keeping his hold on her. She was surprisingly heavy for a small woman.

Two paramedics and a gurney were standing by. Gideon set her down. "She was tied up and dumped in the back of that hallway. There is some pretty foul air down there, and I'm not sure how long she might have been breathing that in. Or what it is. I cut the ties that bound her arms and ankles together so I could get her out. I tried not to jostle her."

The paramedics shone a light in her eyes and did a quick exam while starting an I.V. "Has the family been called? We need to know if she has allergies or medical conditions we should know about."

McQueen stepped over. "Her father has been alerted and is on the way to the hospital. Her cousins, Penny and Nash Camhion, are at the precinct but are not on their way. Ms. Camhion said she has strict instructions not to leave the building. Mr. Camhion is staying with her."

Gideon didn't respond to the question in McQueen's look. He addressed the paramedics. "Hopefully, her father will know. She's a victim of a kidnapping and an assault. We'll need all evidence, clothes, and scrapings done."

The paramedic was already cutting the clothes off Clara. "We'll bag and tag. Let's go."

Gideon wanted to go to the precinct but waited for McQueen to give the orders. It was not the one he wanted.

"Eginhard, go to the hospital. I want to make sure we get fingernail scrapings, a rape kit, and all of her clothes bagged. I've got the forensic team on the way to collect anything else that might help find out who did this to her. I want you to supervise. And don't forget to give them your shirt. There could be trace evidence on you."

Gideon nodded, pushing back the argument he wanted to make. "Yes, sir."

McQueen then stopped. "I'll have two officers escort Ms. Camhion and Mr. Camhion to the hospital. Good?"

Gideon felt relieved. "Good. Thank you."

McQueen nodded. "You'll owe me, Detective. And congrats on your promotion. I can see why they promoted you."

This time he didn't wince. He left the building and took

several deep breaths of fresh air, or as fresh as it got in an alley. He stripped off the shirt and bagged it. He then hopped into the cruiser and made his way to the hospital. Thankfully, there was a shirt that mostly fit him in a bag in the trunk. Likely some officer's gym bag.

Clara was in a room when he got there. He stayed outside the room while the medical staff worked on her. He could see that proper procedure was being followed. Clara's clothes were bagged, including his jacket. Swabs were being taken and scrapings were done. He could only hope Clara had managed to get a few licks in of her own.

"Gunshot wound, upper right side."

Gideon turned. "She was shot?"

"Bullet lodged in her ribs. We'll need an x-ray."

Gideon was taller than the female physician who was cutting the last of her clothing off. He could tell from his position in the hallway that the bullet hole was small. A .22 maybe. It only took a minute for the X-ray technician to come. Clara was awake, but barely. She was mumbling, but it was hard to hear.

The curtain was closed a few moments later, and Gideon stepped away. He pulled his phone out of his pocket. Penny had texted him that they were on their way. The heart emoji made him smile.

It was half an hour later when Hayden arrived. A nurse grabbed him when he arrived and whisked him off. Gideon guessed she was getting Clara's medical history, or what little of it an absent father would know. Shortly after, a couple of forensic analysts arrived. They would collect the samples and log them into evidence. He let them do their job while he continued to watch.

"Gideon."

He turned when he heard Penny call him. She rushed over to him and threw herself into his arms. "You found her."

Gideon held her while Nash followed. Gideon didn't like the look on his friend's face, but he knew now was not the time to question him. "The police found her."

Nash came and slapped him on the shoulder. "That's not how they're telling it at the precinct. Said you found her in a narrow hall behind a bunch of shelves. Said you heard her when no one else did."

Gideon couldn't explain it, so he didn't try. "Dumb luck. I'm just glad we found her. I don't know how much longer she…"

Nash looked at the room behind him. "She could have died."

Gideon nodded. "But she didn't. She's in good hands. The staff gathered as much evidence as they could. It'll be on its way to the lab just as soon as the doctors and nurses are done."

Nash scrubbed his face with his hands. "We owe you."

Gideon dismissed that. "That's crap. I was doing my job. We all were."

Penny hugged him tighter. "It's who you are."

Gideon brushed a soft kiss on her hair. "Yes."

Trenton and Isaac were the last to arrive. They were quiet and simply sat with Nash in the waiting room.

Gideon urged Penny to join them. "I'll need to go back to the precinct. If you want, you can stay here. Trenton and

Isaac will stay with both of you. And there will be officers stationed outside Clara's door."

Penny was torn. "I want to see her. And I want you to stay. But I know you have to work."

Gideon knew he'd be doing paperwork until morning. "You could come with me, and I can find you a quiet place to rest. There are couches in some of the offices. And I can bring you back in the morning. I don't know if Clara will be awake tonight."

Nash agreed. "I'll stay. Penny, you should go with Gideon. The people who did this are still out there."

"But they got what they wanted."

Nash shook his head. "Did they?"

Penny shivered. "I truly hope so."

"So do I. Now go. Tomorrow, you can relieve me, and I'll get some sleep. I'm too wired right now, so I'm better off here."

Trenton urged her, too. "Isaac and I aren't going anywhere. We'll make sure to call if anything changes."

"Okay." Penny grabbed her purse and followed Gideon outside.

Gideon paused to take in the night sky. The rain from the past two days had dissipated, and the skies were clear. "I haven't taken you out on a real date."

Penny tucked her arm into his. "Plenty of time for that. We can go to dinner and go for a walk under the stars."

Gideon opened the door for her. "We seem to be doing things backward."

Penny slid in. "Sounds kinky."

Lust was a sucker punch in his gut, but he tamped it

down. "And you're a vixen. I'll take you up on that later. That I can promise you."

When they got to the precinct, he found an office with a couch for her to sleep on across from the bullpen. She would be within earshot if she needed him. He scrounged up a pillow and blanket from the break room; it wasn't unheard of for a cop to crash at the office. There were a couple of cots set up off the break room if needed. It was called a "wellness" room, but it often was repurposed.

There were other officers from the warehouse doing much the same as he was. Personal field logs would be filled out, and any other observations logged. Since he was the one who found Clara, he wrote a detailed report.

McQueen came in an hour later. "That was good work, Eginhard. I hear she's awake. We're trying to get her to release her medical records, but she's balking. But we have the bullet; it lodged on the surface of her ribs, so the doctor was able to extract it without surgery. The bullet didn't do as much damage as it could have. Not a lot of damage to the bullet either, so we could match ballistics if we find the weapon. And we have DNA samples from her rape kit. Seman was found."

Gideon swore. "I was afraid of that."

McQueen yawned. "I'm going to grab a cup of coffee and join you. It's going to be a long night."

* * *

The hospital was quiet when Penny arrived to visit Clara. Gideon brought her but remained in the hallway as Penny went in. She had to bite back a cry at the look of her cousin. Her lip was busted, there was bruising around both her eyes, and she had part of her hair shaved where stitches were needed to sew up the gash in her head.

Despite how she looked, Clara opened her eyes. "Penny. I'm glad you're here and not Nash. I don't want to see him."

Penny pulled the chair to the bed so she could sit. "He had a feeling you'd say that. Just know he was here all night just outside this door. I just relieved him so he could go get some rest. He wasn't comfortable leaving you here alone."

Clara closed her eyes. "I can't believe this happened. Just like Nash."

Penny's eyes teared up, both at the pain on Clara's face and in her voice, and the painful memories from years ago. "Have you talked to anyone about it?"

Clara turned her head away. "There was already a counselor in here. I'm not interested. I know what was done to me. Nothing I say, nothing they say, is going to change it."

Penny argued. "They can help you cope. To heal."

Clara turned her tear-filled eyes to Penny. "Like they did Nash? No, thanks."

Penny wanted to argue more but didn't think continuing this conversation now, when Clara was still raw and vulnerable, was the right time. Nash hadn't let the counselors and therapists help him. She had hopes Clara would.

Clara turned away once again. "Are there any leads?"

Penny set a hand on Clara's back, trying to soothe her with her touch. "One of the men who took you was the same man who tried to grab me. Dad had security cameras in the house, and they captured the entire abduction."

Clara's voice came out in a squeak. "Cameras? Since when does your house have cameras?"

Penny just kept rubbing her back. "Apparently since three nights before the party. Gideon had suggested Dad put them in. I was with Gideon, and you and Mom were picking up your dresses when Dad had the security team put them in. I'm so glad he did. Now we at least have two faces. It is more than we had. And my police sketch matches one of the men. The larger one with bushy eyebrows."

Clara shifted away. "I didn't see them. They kept my head covered."

Penny's voice choked. "Can you tell me what happened? Where did they take you?"

Clara turned angry eyes on her. "Why? So you can know all the sordid details? I'll tell you what happened. Your family happened. This would never have happened to me if I weren't working for your family. They grabbed me, knocked me on the head, beat me with their fists, and raped me. Is that what you wanted to hear, Penny?"

Penny wasn't sure if it was shock or horror that she felt the most. Shock, because she'd never seen Clara so angry before. Horror at what she had endured at the hands of those men.

"Clara, I'm so sorry."

Clara shoved her hand away. "It was supposed to be you. Get out."

Penny numbly grabbed her purse and quietly left the

room. Gideon held his arms out to her, and she fell into them. She let Gideon lead her away from Clara's room. He didn't take her far, but they had privacy.

Gideon simply held her. "She's going to need help. It's normal to be angry. To place blame on others, and to lash out. She's going to need your love and sympathy through this."

Penny just wept until there were no more tears. "Should I leave her?"

Gideon answered by wrapping his arm around her shoulder and leading her to the elevators. "For now. No matter her reasons, I'm not going to let you be her outlet. Hayden should be back here shortly. Let him try to console her if he can. She is more apt to listen to him than to you, Nash, or your parents right now."

Penny grabbed a tissue from her oversized purse. "It doesn't seem right."

Gideon punched the down button on the elevator. "I know. Nothing about this situation is right. I'll do what I can to find those men. And when she's ready, you'll be there for her. It's all we can do."

"Any more leads?"

Gideon guided her out of the building and to his car. Traffic was light as he pulled out of the hospital parking lot. "DNA is still being processed. I hope we get a match. Penny, I heard what she said to you. The rape kit had DNA to process. At minimum, we have evidence of the assault and can match it."

Penny's eyes darted to him. "You knew about the rape?"

Gideon kept his hands on the steering wheel and his eyes

on the road. "I am not at liberty to discuss the particulars of the case with you. You know that. It was her story to tell."

Penny's eyes went cold. "Not at liberty to discuss? She's my cousin. I know she was beaten; I know she was shot. But you weren't at liberty to discuss the fact that those sick men raped my cousin?"

Gideon took a deep breath. "Penny, it's part of the job. I can't come home and tell you about my day. I don't sit at a desk pushing papers. I deal with people and people's lives. It's confidential. Cousin or not, it's not my right or my place to disclose something like that."

Penny got a hold of her temper. The rape shouldn't shock her. Two sick men had kidnapped her cousin and could do anything they wanted to with her. "I'm going to be sick."

Gideon saw her pale, ashen skin. He heard her gasping for breath. He quickly changed lanes and pulled over. He undid her seat belt and gently pushed her head between her knees. "Deep breaths, Penny. Inhale slowly and exhale just as slowly. Control your breathing. You'll be fine."

Penny did as he asked, letting the sound of his voice take her out of her head for a moment. The dizzy feeling passed, and she didn't feel like she was going to throw up anymore. But the ugly feeling inside her wouldn't fade. "She said it should be me. It should have been me. This wouldn't have happened to her if they had taken me."

Gideon yanked her straight, and his hard gaze bore into hers. "I'm glad it wasn't you. And I'll be damned if I'm going to feel sorry for it. Your being hurt the way she was isn't going to change what happened. Had they gotten a hold of you, they still would have gone after Clara and Victoria. This would still have happened to Clara. This is about Eldridge. I can feel it. None of you are safe. So stop it. And so help me, if I have to yell at you until you believe me, I will."

Penny got a grip on herself. Her voice was soft when she spoke. "You're right. Guilt won't help."

Gideon took a deep breath. He yanked her seat belt back over and buckled her in. He eased back into traffic.

Silence reigned until Gideon pulled into the parking lot of his apartment building.

Penny looked at him. "Still mad?"

Gideon's lips were pursed. "Yeah."

Penny opened her car door. "Okay."

Gideon followed her until they were inside the apartment. "Your response to that is 'okay?'"

Penny turned to him, but this time she was smiling. "Yeah. Just okay. You can be mad at me. Won't be the last time. I was mad at you, though I'm not anymore."

Penny could tell Gideon didn't want to be over his anger yet, but she wrapped her arms around him, and he dropped his forehead to hers.

"The things you do to me." Gideon pulled her in closer.

Penny complied. "It's only fair. You do the same to me. Want to make love to me? You won't be mad anymore."

Gideon swept her up into his arms. "I'm not mad anymore. But I'm feeling randy as hell."

Penny's mouth dropped open. "Is this where we get to the kinky stuff?"

Gideon dropped her on the bed and slammed the door

with his foot as he stripped off his clothes. "Yes."

Penny felt herself melting and started pulling off her own clothes. "Good."

Chapter Thirteen

Penny was humming while she made dinner. Her body was still throbbing from what she considered to be the most intense sex she'd ever had. He'd had her on her stomach and inside her so fast, she'd barely been able to catch her breath. For the next hour, they'd trashed his bed.

"That smells good." Gideon came out of the bathroom, rubbing the moisture from his hair.

"Nothing special. Just putting a casserole together." Penny tipped her neck when Gideon nuzzled it.

"Tomorrow I'm going to go into the precinct. I thought you might want to hang out with Nash."

"At Cantwell? I'd love to." Penny tossed in a handful of spices.

Gideon laughed. "Somehow, I thought you'd like that idea. Trenton can show you his latest photos, and Isaac can sign your book."

Penny waved where she had set it down. "I've barely gotten through the first chapter. This has been the best and worst week of my life."

Gideon stirred what she was frying. "I hope I'm the best part."

Penny shifted between him and the stove. "Best."

Gideon accepted the invitation and initiated the steamy

kiss. "Dinner is going to burn."

Penny slowly pulled back and slid out from between him and the stove. "So practical."

Gideon continued stirring. "One of us has to be. You can be it next time."

Penny planted a wet kiss on his cheek. "Don't expect me to. I'm feeling very impractical."

"Mmm," was Gideon's response.

They were quiet for a while. "So, speaking of practical, it's kicking in. How long do you think this will go on? I mean, I like working. And it doesn't look good to have the head of the company disappear. I had my secretary mark me as out of the office, but I have to get back soon. And honestly, my mom loves her mother-in-law, but only in small doses. Grandma takes a special kind of person to appreciate all her great qualities and not-so-great ones."

Gideon took the pan off the burner. "I thought you meant something else for a minute. I know you can't do all of your work remotely. If we don't find these men, we could assign a bodyguard to escort you. I'll be back on duty soon, and I won't be able to be with you."

Penny saw the vulnerability that came through for a moment. "Gideon. I'm not going anywhere. Though, for the sake of practicality, I think we should at least consider moving into my house. You can have a proper office there. And we'll have more room. Though if you're really attached to the apartment, I do enjoy your oversized bed."

Gideon leaned back on the counter and contemplated her. "You think we should live together? What about after that?"

Penny bit her lip. "I figured you were a one-step-at-a-time kind of guy. I don't want to rush you into anything. But know that if you break up with me, I'll kill you."

Gideon stayed where he was. "Nash might beat you to it. But it's a non-issue. I don't want to rush you."

Penny contemplated that. "Okay, then, let's not rush each other. But we can rush ourselves. I want to get married and make babies. In that order."

Gideon's voice was gruff. "Penny, I think you need to think about this. This happened fast, and at a time when you were vulnerable. Think about who you're talking about marriage and babies with. I'm not the kind of man you need."

Penny flung her arm toward the bedroom. "Need, Gideon? You think I do that with every guy I go out with? You play my body like an instrument, and you're good at it. You make my heart race just looking at you. You make me mad; you make me happy; you make me laugh, and you make me cry. Right now, you're going to make me cry. I know what I want. I don't need to think about it. But maybe you need to figure out what you want. You can get me that bodyguard; I'm going home."

Penny stormed out of the kitchen and into the bedroom. She wiped angry tears from her cheeks. She started throwing her clothes into her suitcase, not caring about anything else but getting away from Gideon. Her heart was breaking because if he didn't know what he wanted and wasn't willing to fight to keep her, then what were they doing?

Gideon appeared in the doorway. "You can't go home.

I'll take you to Nash."

Penny's shoulders slumped. "Fine."

Penny finished packing and Gideon drove her to Cantwell's office. Neither of them said a word. He sat stone still as he drove. Penny fought to fight back tears. He followed her up the stairs, carrying her suitcase. He left her and the suitcase at the door and left when she was safely inside. "Nash!"

Nash came out of his office; his eyes still had dark circles under them, and his hair was in disarray. "What? What are you doing here? Where's Gideon?"

"Heading home. I left him."

Nash swore. "What happened?"

Penny hiccupped. "He doesn't want to marry me and have babies."

Nash's eyes narrowed. "Is that what he said?"

Penny dropped her suitcase. "No. He said I need to be sure. To think it over."

Nash contemplated his sister. "And did you? Think it over?"

Penny slapped her palm on the wall. "I don't need to think it over. He does."

Nash took her hand, soothed the red mark, and pulled her into his office. "So instead of talking it through, you walked. Which is exactly what he's been waiting for you to do."

"So this is my fault?" Penny was half-ready to smack him.

Nash sighed. "Look, I told you to take it easy. That you could hurt him. I have no doubt you're hurting, too, but think of it from his point of view. You're the beautiful princess and he's the tarnished knight. He stayed as far away from you as he could. He kept his distance and tried to make you keep yours. Then you pushed yourself into his life, manipulated his sense of duty, and made him confess that he's in love with you."

Penny rose and slapped both her hands on his desk. "What? I did no such thing."

Nash patted her hands. "I'll take part of the blame. I manipulated his sense of duty. And Mom, too, by sending you to him with those letters. And I admit, finding you two fresh out of bed was what I was hoping to see when I suggested you stay with him. But I didn't think the two of you would go from zero to a hundred in a week. Really, Penny, marriage and babies in one week? What guy wouldn't freak out? And Gideon, being a gentleman, didn't jump at your offer. He wants you to think it over. To be sure. Because if you change your mind, Penny, I don't know if his heart will survive it."

Penny started pacing. "First off, I didn't make him tell me he loved me. He did that all on his own."

Nash twirled his pen, amusement on his face. "Did you say it first?"

"Ha. No, he did."

Nash's eyes narrowed. "What are you not telling me?"

"Okay, I sort of pushed him into it. But he made me mad. And then I made him mad."

"So you rushed it."

"I did not. He said he loved me all on his own. He said he needed me. Why would he not want to marry me?"

Nash set the pen down. "Penny, he wants to marry you. He'd do anything for you. He'd give his life for you. If you had any idea how deep his feelings ran, you might have run away, scared of the depths of them. He's spent his whole life trying to make amends for the night he saved me. I can't tell you why, Penny, but the whole situation scarred him, and I don't mean on the outside."

Penny turned turbulent eyes to her brother. "He told me he had a gun and was going to rob a liquor store." She paused. "Tarnished armor."

Nash nodded. "Yeah. There's a reason he calls me the prince. And I guarantee you're the princess. So when he told you to think it over, that's all he wanted. He wanted you to be sure. Nothing else. No hidden meanings."

"He said he wasn't the man I need."

Nash shrugged. "Maybe. He could be right. But you're the woman he needs. And you left."

Penny sniffled and wiped fresh tears. "So now what do I do?"

Nash pointed to the air mattress. "Get some rest. Let him do his job. You can stay here. The guys are out getting dinner. And when Gideon solves this, and he will, you're going to put on a pretty dress, slather on some makeup, go to his apartment, and wait for him to drop to one knee and propose."

Penny's eyes narrowed. "Slather?"

Nash shrugged. "Goop, slather, smear. Whatever."

"You're going to make some unlucky woman a terrible husband one day."

Nash rose and kissed her on the cheek. "And you are

going to be the most beautiful bride. Give Gideon time. He'll do things his way, and you'll get exactly what you want. I promise."

* * *

Gideon lay on the couch while staring at the ceiling, unable to sleep. He couldn't bear to go into the bedroom. By five, right before the sun came up, he rolled off the couch and went to the precinct. Somewhere in the pile of evidence was the answer to who was behind this.

It was quiet when Gideon arrived, but he had no doubt the analysts would be busy working. They worked in shifts and teams, and someone was always ready to be called in when needed.

"Morning." Gideon poked his head through the door.

Freya, the newest on the team, was at a table. Her blonde hair was tied up in a messy bun, and her eyes looked glazed behind her glasses as she worked. He didn't think she was aware of him until she spoke.

"Detective. What can I do for you?"

"Brooks case. McQueen put a rush on it."

"Mmm. Yes, he did. Quite forcefully. The guy could use a personality transplant. But that's what I'm doing now. Been at it all night."

"Anything back yet?"

"DNA results are back. Database is running the results to see if we get a match. Facial recognition also came back. Good news, we've got your guy. The one who attacked Ms. Camhion."

Gideon's heart raced and adrenaline surged. He took the paper from her. "Damn. I've heard of Parker Monroe. Likes to think of himself as a big player in the city. Wasn't my case."

"Real slime ball, if you ask me. Assault, rape, theft, drugs; you name it. Slap on the wrist each time. Guy has a fancy lawyer. Same one who got the mayor out of hot water last year. Gotta wonder how Parker pays for his services."

Gideon ran through the rap sheet, memorizing its contents. "It's a good question."

"And one I can answer. Latrell traced his financials after we saw who his attorney is. Someone pays him big bucks. We're still tracing the bank account to see who the lucky contestant is." Freya handed him the printout.

Gideon took the paper but didn't look at it. "Okay, and?"

Freya handed him two more sheets. "You know me well. I'm flattered. The first one is known accomplices. Number four looks a lot like your party guy number two. Another loser who calls himself Cortez on the streets. And the GSR test was positive."

"Gunshot residue?" Gideon looked at the result. An expletive was his only response as he ran out of the lab, leaving Freya to shake her head and go back to work.

"You're welcome!"

* * *

Nash and Penny were chatting in the office when the lights went out. Nash fumbled in the dark for a flashlight. "What the hell? Penny, hide."

"Too late." The man's voice echoed in the room. The flashlight he held temporarily blinded the pair.

A second man stood next to him, his gun pointed at Penny.

A woman's voice came from the shadows. "So pathetic."

Nash went down when a taser light flashed and hit him in the chest.

Clara stepped into the room as the lights came back on. "Grab her and let's go. Trenton and Isaac will be back any minute. We want to be long gone."

Penny stood still, no longer seeing the gun pointed at her. "Clara. Why?"

Clara slapped her across the face. "I've wanted to do that for years. Let's go."

Penny struggled but wasn't strong enough to fight the man she recognized as her attacker and Clara's supposed kidnapper. She got a kick into his shin, but he easily overpowered her. She cried out in pain when he jerked her arms back and secured them.

The second man kicked Nash. "What are we going to do with him?"

Clara smiled. "Torch the place."

Penny screamed as the man dragged her from the room. "Nash, wake up!"

Nash didn't move.

* * *

Gideon was at Cantwell's office in record time. Trenton and Isaac were getting out of Trenton's Porsche when the building erupted in flames. Without a word or hesitation, the three men bolted into the building, each intent on getting to their friends.

Gideon called and requested a fire truck and an ambulance. "We have a fire in the warehouse district. Office building, 1785 Escott Street. Unknown number of civilians inside. Requesting backup. Detective Eginhard, badge number 78652."

The three men took the stairs two at a time as they rushed to the top of the building. Gideon halted them when they reached the top. Smoke had not spread to the lower levels, but up here he could barely see. Gideon didn't see anything to protect their faces, but there was a water fountain. Gideon shook off his battered leather jacket and tossed it. He then took off the white dress shirt he was wearing and tore it into pieces. Aggravated with the fountain, he wet the fabric as quickly as he could. "Wrap this over your nose and mouth."

Gideon tossed the fabric without looking. Keeping to the side, he busted the glass and opened the door. "Office."

The three men kept low as the fire continued to spread through the room. Trenton and Isaac followed Gideon's lead.

Trenton spotted Nash first. "There."

Isaac wiped the soot off his glasses so he could see. "He's got a pulse. Grab him."

Trenton and Isaac lifted Nash up by his armpits, dragging him out of the room. Flames licked at them as they made their way out.

Gideon looked around as the flames spread, but there

was no sign of Penny. He could feel the heat intensify and the smoke building. Everywhere he looked, no Penny. His gut clenched. She wasn't here.

Gideon gestured for the two men to go before him. He drew his gun in case someone was waiting for them.

Nash woke to the jostling, his side hurting, and his mouth filled with smoke. He coughed harshly. "Penny. Clara."

Gideon urged them toward the stairs. They made it to the stairwell and down the five flights of stairs in record time. Paramedics were standing by as the fire crew arrived. Gideon yelled at the fire crew. "No one is on the top floor. Other offices should be empty at this hour, but I can't be sure."

The men geared up as Gideon turned to find Trenton and Isaac helping Nash onto the gurney while the paramedics were placing oxygen on him.

Nash thrashed, fighting to get the mask off. "Clara."

Isaac glanced at Gideon. "She should be safe at the hospital."

Gideon kept his eyes on Nash. "Clara is behind the kidnapping."

Nash coughed and continued to fight. "Clara. Penny. Tracker in Penny's purse."

Gideon realized what Nash was saying. "I've got to get the security team on the phone. Penny has a tracker in her purse. Clara has Penny. You two stay with Nash."

Nash stopped fighting and slumped back. "Save her."

Gideon clutched Nash's hand in a fist. "I swear I will."

* * *

Penny tried to see where they were going, but the back of the van she was stashed in had the windows covered. So far, no one had truly hurt her; she didn't count Clara's slap.

How could she not have seen it? She worked side by side with Clara for years. Clara and her mom loved to shop together. Clara was at every family event. Penny thought of her as a sister. But a sister would never betray the family the way Clara had.

"Nothing to say, Penny?" Clara taunted her from the front seat. The man with the bushy eyebrows drove, while the smaller man sat in the back with a gun on her.

"Why?" Penny heard the question pop out before she could pull it back.

"That is the question. I might satisfy your curiosity. But it might just kill you." Clara laughed from the front seat.

Penny tried to relax her muscles, ignoring Clara, who was still laughing. She needed to be ready to bolt the second an opportunity arose. She knew for certain Clara had every intention of killing her. Tears burned Penny's eyes. She could only pray Nash was still alive. She had watched in horror as the smaller man poured gasoline all over the room before flicking a match. The room had gone up in a rush of flames. Bushy Eyebrows yanked her from the room as she screamed Nash's name.

Clara pointed. "There. Pull around the back. We don't want anyone to see us from the street."

The small man yanked Penny to her feet. "Move."

Penny stumbled and fell as he pushed her from the van.

Her knees hit the concrete, and pain seared through her legs.

"Now, now. Be nice to my cousin. She's about to have a rough day." Clara shoved her forward as she stumbled to her feet.

Penny swallowed hard when she realized they were in her backyard. Her two-story home stood empty, lights off and doors secured. She saw Clara open her purse and take out her key. She unlocked the door and undid the alarm. Penny silently cursed. Clara was one of her emergency contacts and had the security codes for her home.

"Come, cousin. I already disposed of your phone, so no one can track you here. And no one will ever know I'm the one behind this."

Penny walked backward into her kitchen. "I don't understand. We love you. You're family."

Clara shoved her hard against the fridge. "Family! You don't know the meaning of the word. Your family ruined mine. My father left, and it's because of your father. Eldridge did this. He ruined my father's reputation and ruined the business deal that was going to make us rich. Richer than Eldridge."

Penny blinked her eyes to try to clear her head from where it had hit the fridge. "Your father botched the deal, stole the investors' money, and took off. My father didn't do that. Yours did."

Clara slapped her harder this time. "My father told me what happened. Your family took me in; acted like you were doing me a favor. But you used me; Eldridge used me to build up Camhion. But I'll be the one in charge when you're gone. Nash is dead. And you will be soon. In their grief, Victoria and Eldridge will turn the business over to me. The fifty million I got from Nash will be chump change in comparison to what I'll own. Then one day, Victoria and Eldridge will make me their sole heir, and won't it be so tragic when I'm forced to take over when they die in an unfortunate accident."

Penny could taste blood in her mouth. "You're crazy."

"Maybe." Clara conceded. "But my plan is perfect."

Clara then waved to the two men. "Go get things set up. I'll finish this."

Penny tried to reason with her. "No plan is perfect. The police have pictures of those two men. They'll spill their guts. The police have some of their DNA."

Clara pulled a gun out of her pocket. It was a .22. "No, they don't."

Penny's eyes were on the gun. "Yes. They collected the semen sample."

"Oh, please. You don't think I can get laid when I want? Men are so easy. Including those two out there. The police have the DNA of some random guy I picked up in a bar. He's going to have quite the time explaining how his DNA got inside a kidnapping and rape victim, assuming he's ever found."

"But you were beaten, shot, and assaulted. Why? Why not just kidnap me and be done with it? Why the ruse?"

Clara waved the gun to get Penny to move into the living room. "Because men are idiots, that's why. The two morons out there grabbed me instead of you. We were both wearing blue silk. We both had our hair up in a twist.

People always say we looked like sisters. They tossed a towel over my head and dragged me out instead of you. I was forced to make a new plan. But this works nicely. No one will think I beat myself up or shot myself, no matter what evidence the cops might find. And there were signs of sexual assault, the sex part anyway. And when I shoot you and leave the gun behind, the ballistics from the bullet in my chest will match the ones they find in you. No one will suspect I had anything to do with it. Even your boyfriend hasn't figured it out."

"Yes, he has." Gideon stood in the doorway, his weapon drawn and pointed straight at Clara's heart.

Clara turned, but the gun was steady on Penny. "Isn't that sweet. Killing a cop wasn't in the plans. But I'll adjust."

McQueen stepped into the room, circling until she was flanked. "Except you'd have to kill two. Drop the weapon, Ms. Brooks. It's over."

Clara's scream echoed through the room as her finger tightened on the trigger. "It's not over!"

Gideon took the shot that ended Clara's life.

* * *

Gideon opened his arms when Penny ran to him. He caught her up, kissed her, and vowed to never let her go. "You have no idea how scared I was."

"Same." She turned frightened eyes to his. "Nash?"

"Alive. He's in the hospital for side effects from a taser and smoke inhalation. But he'll be okay. We got to him as fast as we could."

Penny pressed her face to his chest. "We?"

Gideon pulled back so he could see her face. "Trenton and Isaac. They are the ones who carried him out."

McQueen holstered his gun. "I'd really like to know how you determined Clara was behind it."

Gideon tucked Penny to his side. "GSR test was positive."

"What GSR test?"

Gideon explained. "For reasons I don't know, Clara was swabbed for GSR."

Penny interrupted. "GSR?"

McQueen brushed that off. "Gunshot residue. But she was the one who was shot, not the shooter."

Gideon shook his head. "She was both. My guess is that Monroe and Cortez beat her up. And one of them had sex with her; hence the semen, but she shot herself."

Penny interjected. "Clara said she had sex with some guy she picked up in a bar to throw the police off the trail of the real kidnappers."

McQueen grunted. "That would have put a kink in the investigation for sure. What else?"

Gideon continued. "Large cash payments were made directly to Monroe from an offshore account. Forensics hadn't traced the bank account to an owner yet, but I would bet good money Clara's name, or an alias that can be tied to her, will be on it. Nash's money wired to Clara's account from our account has already been found. She transferred it to an offshore account, but our team tracked it."

Penny was shocked. "But how did you find me?"

Gideon smiled down at her. "Nash. He put a tracker in your purse. According to the security company, he had one on him, too. He even slipped one into Clara's bag, though it didn't help since her bag was still at the house when she was taken. Nash wanted to make sure the three of you could be found should something happen. Cell phones can be shut off or tossed. Not as easy when you're being tracked and don't know it."

Penny shivered. "So which one is Monroe, and which one is Cortez? And where are they? Did they run?"

McQueen gestured to the back yard. "Nope. I brought backup. They are in police custody. All either of them will say right now is 'lawyer' but we have video footage of them kidnapping Clara, or at least what we thought was an abduction, and you identified Monroe as your attacker. We don't need to worry as much about the poor bastard Ms. Brooks tried to frame, though we'll want to find him if we can, so the defense attorney can't cry foul. This one is one hell of a mess."

Gideon could only agree. "I'll turn in my gun and badge until the investigation into Clara's shooting is done. But I'm glad you were a witness to it, Detective."

McQueen shrugged. "We'll both be stuck with the paperwork. But such is our life as detectives. Why don't you drop Ms. Camhion at the hospital so she can see her brother and then come back to the station? I'll put on the coffee."

Chapter Fourteen

"For the hundredth time, I'm fine," Nash grumbled while Penny fussed.

Trenton snickered. "Just glad it's you and not me, pal. Though I wouldn't mind a little fussing. I did scrape my knuckles lugging you out of that building. Singed my hair, too."

Isaac pushed his glasses higher up on his nose. "I lost the tab on my glasses, and they keep slipping off my nose."

Trenton raised his fist. "We both need sympathy."

Penny and Nash were both laughing. But halfway through, Penny burst into tears.

Trenton immediately went to her. "Oh man, Penny, don't do that. Nash is fine. We're fine. Gideon is fine."

Penny shook as she succumbed to the stress of the night. Seeing Clara shot was something she would live with for a long time. "And Clara is dead. I can't believe Clara was behind this."

Nash took her hand. "I'd console you, but it hurts to breathe. Why don't you go find Gideon? I wish I had an answer for you on Clara. But I don't know if we will ever understand. None of us saw it."

Isaac shrugged. "Never liked her, myself. Do the police think her father had something to do with this?"

Trenton seconded that. "She didn't strike me as being particularly clever. Seems pretty suspect that Clara pulled this off all by herself. Well, except for Joker One and Joker Two."

Penny looked at Nash. "She didn't mention her father once. And he had an alibi for the time Clara was snatched. He seemed genuinely shocked. I don't know where he is now, but I would think he's at the police station. They'll investigate him, right?"

"No doubt. But if they don't, Dad will." Nash coughed and struggled for a moment to catch his breath.

Penny wiped the tears from her cheeks. "You need to rest. Talking can't be good for your throat."

Nash closed his eyes. "What I wouldn't give for a good glass of bourbon right now. Probably burn like hell, though. Why don't all of you go home and sleep in your comfy beds? I think we're all sick of air mattresses. When I get out of here, we have a lot of work to do. Cantwell burned tonight."

Penny thought back to the drawings Gideon did. She held back tears at the lost work. "All of your hard work."

Isaac shook his head. "Not all of it. I have the soft copy of my novel. I'll get more books printed. Just think, Penny, you have the only first edition copy. Going to be worth money someday. But Delilah has all the artwork and storyboards at her apartment, so it's not a complete wash."

That perked Penny up. "She has it all at her place? Why?"

Trenton nudged Isaac. "Yeah, Isaac, why?"

Isaac gave Trenton a dirty look. "She said she couldn't

spend another moment listening to me drone and lecture. Then she said there was way too much testosterone in the room for her to concentrate. She packed everything up to work on it at her apartment while we camped out at Cantwell's office. Said she wasn't coming back until we moved out."

Trenton laughed. "Yep. Isaac bored her to death, Nash kept arguing with her over colors, and she seemed immune to my many charms. So she left."

"Charms." Penny smiled for the first time in hours. "That's great. I'm going to go find Gideon. Love you all!"

Penny tucked her purse under her arm and had to tell herself to walk, not run, to her car. She had plans for Gideon.

*　*　*

The sun was coming up when Gideon unlocked the door to his apartment. He had thought of driving straight to Penny's but wasn't sure about the reception he'd get, assuming she wasn't still at the hospital with Nash. She'd run to him after he'd shot Clara, and he'd done his best to lessen the horror of seeing her cousin shot dead. But she had been silent on the way to the hospital, and he hadn't known what to say to her. He knew seeing her cousin shot and killed was a memory that would haunt her for a long while. Seeing a gun held on Penny would haunt him for the rest of his life. Because she hadn't spoken to him and barely looked at him on the way to Nash, he left her with Nash, Trenton, and Isaac instead of trying to talk to her. She couldn't be in better hands. And he knew seeing her brother would help ease some of the trauma of the night. And with her parents on their way home, she'd have all the support she needed.

He shivered a little as he went and turned up the heat. His beloved black leather jacket had been lost in the fire, and the only things he had on were jeans and an undershirt. He stunk like smoke and looked like he'd been sucker-punched; the dark circles were so bad under his eyes. He hadn't slept after Penny had left him. He'd just tossed and turned on the couch. And he hadn't gotten any sleep since. Once he'd seen the GSR test and the puzzle pieces dropped into place, it had been a marathon of a day.

First things first, he needed a shower. Then he needed food. Then he needed to figure out how to fix things with Penny. He still wasn't sure why he didn't leap at the offer when she said she wanted to get married and have babies. In truth, he hadn't given much thought to children. He liked them well enough, though he didn't know the first thing about taking care of them. He had never even had a pet to practice on.

But despite the surge of lust at the thought of Penny pregnant with his baby, a part of him still held back. He wanted Penny. He loved her. And he believed she loved him. But love wasn't enough. He didn't believe in love songs and poetry. People had to work at it. It didn't just happen, and things weren't always rainbows and roses. He knew he had his moods. He was quick to anger, though not violent with it. He brooded a lot; sometimes over work, sometimes over the things he wished he could change but couldn't. His relationship with Penny, at least the intimate one, was too new, too fragile. He wanted to plow ahead and rush her to the altar. But that wasn't the right way to go about it. He didn't need time; there was nothing about Penny he didn't desire. She was light and good and kind. He wasn't. And for nothing in the world did he want to dim that light.

And that's why he'd said what he'd said. She needed to be sure. He needed her to be sure she wanted forever, till death do they part, and not just something said in the heat of the moment. But the second he'd dropped her off at Cantwell, he knew he'd made a huge mistake. Penny wasn't like the other women he'd dated. She was like his mother and sister. She knew her own mind. She wasn't afraid to say what she wanted. But he'd been afraid to go back, to mess things up more than he already had.

Contemplating his next steps, Gideon stripped and tossed his clothes in the washer. He didn't want the smoke smell permeating the apartment. He scrubbed down in the shower until his skin was red. Then not bothering to get dressed, he went into the kitchen. There wasn't anything appetizing inside the fridge. He closed the door and laid his forehead against the door.

"Eginhard, you're an idiot." Gideon spoke the words aloud, knowing that it was nothing but the truth.

"Gideon, for goodness' sake, get in here. You are taking way too long."

Gideon lifted his head. "Penny?"

The words were muffled. "It better be, or you're in trouble."

Gideon looked at his bedroom door, a door that was never closed. His heart pounding, he opened the door. He gasped when he saw her.

Penny looked annoyed as she lay in his bed, candles burning on the end tables, and rose petals on the sheets.

Gideon stared in shock. Penny was dressed in a white silk negligee with her hair piled on top of her head. One strap hung over a creamy shoulder. The garter belt he could see peeking out from under the lace trim was almost his undoing. He'd never seen anything so sexy in his life as Penny lying on his bed, waiting for him.

Penny gave him a knowing smile. "Happy to see me?"

Gideon realized he was standing naked in the doorway. "I'm going to ask the obvious. What are you doing here?"

Penny sat up and came to her knees. "I shouldn't have left. I'm sorry."

Gideon dropped his gaze. "I didn't give you the right answer."

Penny walked on her knees to the edge of the bed. "You gave the right answer for you. If I hadn't been hurt, I'd have realized that. Being in love is scary. I never realized how much until this week. I was scared, wondering if this would work. I was scared because I wanted this so much. I was scared that it wasn't real. And when you said I should think about it, you were right. When you said you weren't the right man for me, well, I beg to differ. You're perfect for me. You're caring, you do what's right, your work is to help others, and you defend the weak. You gave up everything to be with me. To keep me safe. You didn't have to. Even if Nash begged and pleaded, you didn't have to. You did because that's who you are. And I love everything about you, even your moods, and I wouldn't change a thing. So I thought about it. A lot. I want you, Gideon; however way, any way, that you want me."

"Penny." Gideon didn't know what to say to her. So he did what he had only ever dreamed of doing. He came over to the bed. He took her hands and brought her to him until she was standing before him. Then he dropped to one knee.

Penny giggled. Then she giggled again. "I'm sorry, Gideon. Most men have clothes on when they propose."

Gideon did not appreciate the laughter. "Can I get on with this?"

Penny sobered, but her lips were pursed while she held in her giggles. "Yes."

"Penelope Camhion, will you marry me?"

Penny's laughter faded, and her eyes teared up. "Yes."

Gideon scooped her up and set her back on the bed. He came down beside her. "I love you, Penny."

Penny smiled and touched her fingers to his lips. "I love you, too."

Gideon bent to kiss her, but Penny turned her head so she could whisper in his ear. "Can we do that kinky thing again?"

Gideon slid his hands under the hem of her nightgown, exposing the garter. He slipped a finger under it. "I have a better idea."

When Penny was breathless a short time later, she could only agree.

And then...

Trenton Armstrong juggled the donuts and coffee as he climbed the flight of stairs to the new Cantwell office. Nash had finally gone and bought a house, turning the second story into the quartet's new business headquarters. Penny pretended annoyance when the house Nash bought was the one across the street from hers, but Nash had always admired it, and when it had gone up for sale, even Penny couldn't convince him not to buy it. She'd used every sister excuse in the book, but Nash had ignored them and made a generous offer that the owners jumped at before he could change his mind.

"I brought snacks." Trenton turned the corner at the top of the stairs to find Gideon and Penny in a clinch. "Not again. It's like watching your parents."

Penny jumped at Trenton's voice; Gideon glared.

Trenton held up the box that balanced the coffee. "A little help here, Eginhard."

Gideon took the box. "Just what you need. More sugar."

Trenton had a sweet tooth and wasn't afraid to admit it. "I was deprived as a child. What can I say?"

Gideon gave him a sideways glance.

Trenton smiled at him, all teeth. Truth was, there were a lot of things he didn't have as a child. Deprived was probably not quite the right word, but it was all he had. The quartet knew him best. And they knew he used humor to mask the darkness that still lived inside him after all these years. The outward world saw the class clown; a guy who didn't take life seriously. Trenton much preferred that to the truth.

Shaking off his mood, he smiled at the couple. He was overjoyed for both of them. Everyone knew Gideon was in love with Penny. And Trenton had been quite sure Penny was in love with him, too. To see them together, always touching or kissing, made him happy. And he'd been honored when Gideon had asked for his help picking out a ring.

Trenton took a large donut out of the box. "Okay, so we have a date set. Though I'm still in shock that Victoria is letting the two of you get away with a small wedding. What's the plan?"

Penny kissed Gideon. "Family only. Just how I want it. And we'll let you come too, Trenton."

Trenton clutched his chest. "Ouch, Penny. After all we've been through together."

Gideon gave him a dirty look. "Watch it, Armstrong. I know how to hide a body."

Trenton grabbed the cup of coffee that he loaded with sugar. He held up both hands in mock surrender. "So two weeks, huh? I'll be sure to dust off my powder-blue tuxedo for the occasion."

Nash snuck up behind him, grabbed a coffee, and eyed the donuts. "That I would pay to see. My mother might faint at the sight, though."

Isaac took the comment seriously. "She has a very delicate disposition."

Trenton sipped his coffee and went to the storyboard he had put together last night when sleep eluded him. "So what do you think?"

Penny laid a hand on his shoulder. "I think what I always

think. That you should be selling your photographs instead of giving them away."

Trenton shrugged. "Just a hobby. The stock market is where it's at, baby."

Penny squeezed his shoulder and let it go. "Speaking of, aren't you supposed to be working today, making millions?"

Trenton's eyes closed. "I quit."

All four pairs of eyes turned on him. Isaac, the practical one, admonished him. "That was incredibly irresponsible. You have a mortgage and bills to pay like the rest of us."

Trenton cocked an eyebrow at him. "So my uncle said. I'm going freelance."

That got the attention and approval of the group. Gideon slapped him on the back. "Congrats. You've only been talking about it for five years. Maybe Nash will let you rent office space in his attic."

That started a conversation about how they would decorate it. Some of the suggestions were hilarious. Trenton took another sip of his coffee, watching the people he loved most in the world playfully argue about what color to paint his office. Trenton sipped and listened. Then the darkness inside reared its head, and he thought, perhaps black. To match the color of my soul. Trenton sighed inwardly, forcefully brushed off the mood, then joined in with his own ridiculous ideas, pushing the darkness back where it belonged.

<u>From The Author</u>

This is my eleventh full-length novel. Doesn't seem so long ago that I published my first one, This Time Love. But time sure does fly. Falling Slowly is book one of four in a series I titled The Cantwell Quartet.

To start, I love video games. There is something satisfying when you can adventure and save the world. Or maybe just farm and raise a family. The idea for a new quadrilogy (Isaac featured in book 3 would call it a "tetralogy") started brewing while I was playing an RPG (role-playing game for those of you unfamiliar). It wasn't so much the storyline that inspired me as it was the interaction of the four main characters. The story centers around four men: the prince, the protector, the peacemaker, and the comedian. Not sure that is how the game writers thought of them, but that's how I see them. The four men fight side by side to save the kingdom, and ultimately, the world. Each has their flaws. Each has secrets and pain. And each of them does what's right. My kind of heroes!

I hesitate to name the game for two reasons. One, the books are not based on the storylines in the game, so I don't want to disappoint fans who think they're getting a fan fiction, modern-day book version of the game. The books are my stories with my interpretation of who these men could be in modern day. And two, it's more fun to keep you guessing. But if you guess right, I'll tell you.

Also, if you enjoyed this book, or any of my other titles, please consider leaving a rating at your favorite retailer, Goodreads and/or Bookbub. And if you have the time, a text review would be lovely. Indie authors rely on readers like you to tell others how much you enjoy their books.

Happy reading,

Chapter One

"Excuse me, Miss?"

Jenna "Mac" Mackenzie had to stifle her annoyance. One day she'd learn to take a flight home instead of the cruise ship. Too bad she was terrified of flying. But right now, she was tired and hungry, and the passengers who had just boarded were not her problem.

She turned to the man, intending to tell him no, but then did a second take. The man was tall and lanky, though his shoulders looked broad enough under the oversized Hawaiian shirt he was wearing. His legs were long and lean, like those of a runner. She had a nice view of them under his board shorts. He had a handsome, chiseled face, but what threw her was the oversized glasses that he had to keep pushing up his nose from the sweat that was gathering under the plastic frames. He looked like a man trying to fit the part of a vacationer but didn't quite pull it off. He reminded her of a college professor. Or maybe a high school English teacher. A sexy one.

"Yes?" She looked up into his deep brown eyes. A woman could drown in their deep depths; they were so dark, despite the glare on the clear lenses from the bright sun overhead.

"I don't suppose you work here?"

Her mouth twisted in a wry smile. She was a sucker every time. And she supposed she did work here. "I do. Can I help you?"

The tall man took a step closer. "I was wondering if you could help me."

Jenna saw the man's pale skin turn a little green. Figures. He was seasick and they'd barely gotten underway. It wasn't often a man caught her attention, so she continued to let her eyes wander. She was on vacation, after all, and he was cute. But she had no use for men without sea legs. Too bad.

She gestured toward the stern. "I'll get you fixed up. First time on a ship?"

The man followed her as her long, tanned legs ate up the distance between there and sick bay. "That obvious?"

Jenna climbed the stairs to the upper deck. "Sorry, but yes."

She opened the door to sick bay and pulled the tissue paper over the exam chair. "Have a seat."

The man sank into the chair, his pallor still green. "What's the prescription? Antihistamines?"

She glanced over at him as she pulled a box out of the cabinet without looking at it. "Did you throw up?"

He shook his head and turned a darker shade. "Not yet."

Since he wasn't complaining, she let herself feel a little sympathy. "I don't like drugs, unless they're all that helps. We'll fix you up with the wristbands. If they don't work, I'll give you pills to take with you to try. You can get more at the gift shop."

The man took the box from her so he could read it. "Acupressure, huh?"

She could tell he was skeptical. "It helps some people. Not everyone. But it's better than a pill that will make you tired. You're on a cruise ship with the most beautiful view in the world. You don't want to sleep through it."

The man handed her back the box and looked her in the eyes. "It is a beautiful view."

Jenna stared at him. He looked to be memorizing her face. It was a cheesy line, but the look that accompanied it made her heart beat a little faster.

She cleared her throat. "Right. Thanks. You wear them like this so that the pressure is on the inside."

He watched as she took them out and adjusted them. "They're pink."

She huffed a little. "Not manly enough to wear pink?"

The man laughed, which was not the reaction she was expecting. "I guess I'm going to find out."

Jenna took a step back. "Seasickness may or may not pass. I'll get you a couple of packs of the pills in case the wristbands don't help."

He stayed where he was sitting, his eyes on her.

She pulled a couple of packs out and handed them to him. "Here you go. Instructions on the back, but hopefully it won't come to that."

The man tucked them into his pocket. "Thank you, Miss—"

"Jenna." She gave him her real name instead of the nickname everyone else called her.

"I appreciate it, Jenna. I'm Sean Cameron."

Oh, boy. Jenna knew that name. That was the name of the client who had hired her to take him out into the Florida waters to search for some old sunken ship. She had hitched a ride on the cruise ship to beat her client back to the office. She'd been visiting her grandparents and was on her way home. She hoped he found his sea legs. Otherwise, he might cancel on her. Though given her reaction to him, that might not be a bad thing. She didn't consort with clients. She didn't really consort at all. She simply didn't have the time. But he made her think of moonlight kisses and walks on the beach.

She took a step back when Sean slid off the chair. "You might also want to get a little something in your stomach if you haven't eaten. Nothing heavy. And if you do throw up, stay in your cabin. The cool air will help."

He followed her outside, back into the bright sunshine. "Can you point me in the direction of the restaurant?"

Jenna found herself leading the way. "Come on. It can take a little while to get your bearings."

He walked beside her this time, instead of behind. "What do I owe you for the bands and the pills?"

He did look a bit silly in the hot pink bands. She hadn't looked at the color when she'd pulled them out. "On the house, since it's your first cruise. And the ship's maiden voyage, at that."

He mumbled a thank you as they entered the covered restaurant. It was open-air, but the shade would get him out of the sun.

"Hi, Paul. Two cups of potato soup and a couple of baguettes for my friend and me."

"Sure thing, Mac."

"You don't have to watch over me." Sean followed Jenna as she led him to a small table.

Jenna caught his annoyed tone. "What? Don't want to share lunch with me?"

He dropped into a chair. "I'd think you wouldn't want to share lunch with me. I assume you're on the clock."

Jenna flipped her long golden braid over her shoulder. "I'm not working during this voyage, though I do work for the cruise company. I'm on my way home."

Paul dropped off the two cups of soup and bread. "Anything else?"

Jenna thanked him. "We're good. Thanks."

Sean eyed the cup of soup. "Cream can't be good for a sour stomach."

Jenna spooned up a bite. "Perhaps not. But the potatoes are. And the bread. Other than crackers, I'm not sure what else might be in the kitchen."

Sean fished out a bite of potato. He ate it. Waited. Then took another. "This is good."

Jenna tore off a chunk of the bread and soaked it in her soup. "So, what brings you on a cruise ship?"

Sean mirrored her and tried the bread. "My parents. It's their fortieth wedding anniversary. Mom wanted to go on a cruise. Dad grumbled but gave in. It's easier to let Mom have her way.

Mom saw this ship in an ad and thought it was perfect. It's a small ship and it doesn't sail too far out into the ocean."

"And you came with them?"

He nodded as he ate another piece of bread. "Mom insisted since I paid for it. Never mind that it cost more for me to come, but she wouldn't take no for an answer."

Jenna found she liked the timbre of his voice. He had a bit of an East Coast accent, but it wasn't prominent. She guessed he lived there but wasn't born there. "You're not sharing a room with them, are you?"

Sean made a face. "Gross. No."

Jenna giggled. "Good."

Sean leaned back in his seat. "I feel better. Thank you, Jenna."

She leaned back in her seat. "You're welcome."

Want more? The Babe & The Librarian is available now!

www.ingramcontent.com/pod-product-compliance
Lightning Source LLC
Chambersburg PA
CBHW020800310726
48969CB00002B/629